Experience all the chills of the Mostly Ghostly series!

Mostly Ghostly #1: *Who Let the Ghosts Out?*
Mostly Ghostly #2: *Have You Met My Ghoulfriend?*
Mostly Ghostly #3: *One Night in Doom House*
Mostly Ghostly #4: *Little Camp of Horrors*
Mostly Ghostly #5: *Ghouls Gone Wild*

AND COMING SOON:

Mostly Ghostly #6: *Let's Get This Party Haunted!*

R.L. STINE

DELACORTE PRESS

A PARACHUTE PRESS BOOK

Published by
Delacorte Press
an imprint of
Random House Children's Books
a division of Random House, Inc.
New York

A Parachute Press Book

Visit us on the Web! www.randomhouse.com/kids
Educators and librarians, for a variety of teaching tools,
visit us at www.randomhouse.com/teachers

Library of Congress Cataloging-in-Publication Data
is available upon request.

ISBN: 0-385-74692-X (trade)
0-385-90930-6 (lib. bdg.)

Printed in the United States of America

April 2005

10 9 8 7 6 5 4 3

PROLOGUE

MY NAME IS MAX DOYLE, and some scary things have been happening to me.

To begin with, something followed me when I was walking home from hanging out with my best friend, Aaron, at his house. I don't think it was human. I think it was a ghost.

And it wasn't friendly.

The sun had set. Dark storm clouds hung low in the sky. The wind howled around me as I started to walk the two blocks to my house.

I kept my head down and walked with my hands in my pockets. How did it suddenly get so cold? I wondered.

I walked past a few houses—and that's when I heard a scraping sound behind me.

I spun around. Anyone there?

I saw a blur of motion. Something moved behind a low hedge.

I shrugged and started walking again. But now I was listening carefully.

And again, I heard a scrape. A few soft thuds. The sound of footsteps.

Someone was definitely following me.

I stopped. And the sounds behind me stopped too.

I spun around. Hard to see anything in this pitch-black night.

The dark clouds seemed to lower over me. The wind howled and shook the trees.

A chill tightened the back of my neck.

I heard a cough from behind a nearby pine tree.

"Aaron?" I called, shouting over the wind. "Hey—Aaron? Is that you?"

A head poked out from behind the tree.

I squinted in the heavy darkness, trying to see the face.

A boy?

"Is that you, Aaron?" My voice came out shaky and high. My throat suddenly felt tight.

He stepped away from the tree. Yes. A boy. But not Aaron. A boy dressed all in black.

He took a few steps toward me. His face was hidden in shadow. Then moonlight washed over him and I saw his face clearly.

An old man's face! Eyes deep in their sockets. Skin pale and sagging. Mouth turned down in a furious scowl.

A boy with an old man's face!

I turned and ran. My legs felt wobbly and weak. It was hard to keep them moving.

I could hear his pounding footsteps. He was coming after me!

What did he want? Why was he chasing me?

I didn't stop to find out. Gasping for breath, I forced myself to run harder.

I ducked my head as large raindrops began to patter down. The sidewalk ended. I darted across the street. Only half a block to go.

I heard his footsteps on the pavement behind me. He was catching up. He looked like an old man, but he was running as fast as a boy!

Leaning forward, I tried to burn more speed. But I could barely breathe.

And then I let out a cry as my feet slid out from under me. No way to stop myself. I fell hard. Facedown. In a deep muddy trench.

"Oww!"

Gasping, choking, I struggled to my knees. And stared up at the figure in black, his face covered in darkness.

"Who are you?" I cried. "What do you want?"

Silence. He didn't move. The only sounds now were my wheezing breaths and the pelting of raindrops all around.

And then finally, he whispered, whispered in a low, hoarse voice, *"I'm watching . . . I'm watching . . ."*

1

SKIP TO THE NEXT DAY. I didn't have time to think about the creepy boy in black. Why? Because the biggest day of my life was coming up. And that was all I could think about.

"Easy, boy. Easy."

I slid the leash off our dog, Buster, and backed away. "Easy, boy."

Buster stared up at me with his evil red eyes. He's a big, furry wolfhound, and it's my job to take him for a walk in the afternoon.

He pulled back his lips, showed his teeth, and growled. He was trying to decide which part of my body would make a tasty snack. My problem with Buster is he thinks I'm a chew toy.

Luckily, the dog turned away and trotted to the back of the yard. I started into the house, but the kitchen door swung open, and my brother, Colin, burst out.

"Hey, fat face," he said. "I read this new book you'll like."

"Don't call me fat face," I said.

"It's called *Don't Hurt Me,* by I. Bruce Eazly."
Colin let out a loud donkey laugh. "Think fast,
Max!" he shouted.

I didn't have time to move. He swung his arm
back and heaved a bright red Frisbee at my head.

I tried to duck. Not fast enough. The Frisbee
clonked me hard on the forehead.

Next thing I knew, I was flat on my back in the
grass. The sky was spinning above me, and red
and yellow stars were twinkling above my head.

Colin laughed again. "Good catch, ace!" he
said. He pulled me to my feet. "You shoulda
read that book, Maxie. You're gonna have a
big bruise."

"A bruise? But I'm on TV tomorrow!" I cried.
You know I'm giving the school trophy to the
mayor tomorrow."

"That's gonna swell up really huge," Colin
said. "It will show up nice and big on TV. Mayor
Stank won't be able to see your face. He'll think
you're some kind of mushroom life."

I sighed. "Oh, wow. How could you *do* that to
me, Colin?"

"Just trying to play a little Frisbee, punk,"
Colin said. "Having fun with my kid brother."

He gave me a friendly slap on the back—so
hard that he left fingerprints.

"You're just jealous," I said. "Because I'm going to be on TV and you're not."

Colin grinned at me. "Yeah. You got that right," he said. "I'm real jealous of you. Know why?"

"Why?" I said.

"I'm jealous because Buster likes you so much."

He turned and cupped his hands around his mouth. Then he shouted to the dog, "Get him, Buster! Get him, boy! Get Max!"

I staggered back as Buster came galloping across the grass. Panting with excitement, the huge beast leaped into the air. He sank his teeth into my neck and threw me down to the ground with his heavy front paws.

"My throat!" I gasped, trying to wrestle the dog off me. "Help! He's got me by the throat!"

I saw the kitchen door swing open. Dad poked his head out.

"Help!" I cried.

"Max, come in for dinner!" Dad shouted. "And stop teasing the dog!"

2

AFTER DINNER, I WENT up to my room to practice my speech.

I'd been practicing for days, but I really wanted to get it right. Tomorrow was the dedication of the new swimming pool at Jefferson Elementary. And I—Max Doyle—was giving the official school trophy to Mayor Stank, who helped raise money to build the pool. What an honor!

Why was I picked to give the trophy? Because I'm at the top of my sixth-grade class.

The kids all call me Brainimon because I'm the class brain. Tomorrow the whole school would watch me give the trophy to the mayor at the new pool. And the ceremony would also be on Channel 600, our local TV station.

At dinner, Mom said, "I hope all this attention doesn't give you a swelled head, Max."

But of course, I already had a *real* swelled head, thanks to Colin!

In my room, I went over my speech again and again. "Mayor Stank, thank you for helping us all make a real splash. I'm honored to give you this silver trophy . . ."

My computer bleeped. I saw that I had an instant message from Aaron.

"R U nervous?" he asked.

I typed back: "Who? Me? No way."

Aaron probably knew I was lying. He's a pretty smart kid, even though he's a little weird.

How is he weird? Well, for one thing, he always wears swim goggles to school. And he keeps them on all day. And he only wears shorts, never long pants. Even when it's ten degrees out and his legs are turning blue.

Kinda weird, right? But he's the only best friend I've got.

"Y don't U do a magic trick for the mayor?" Aaron wrote. "Make his hat disappear or something. That would be totally cool!"

I'm really into magic. I want to be a great magician someday. And I'd love to do a magic trick on TV.

But I decided tomorrow was not the right time for it.

I typed back to Aaron: "I don't think he wears a hat."

Aaron disappeared. He always does that. He never says goodbye or anything. Just vanishes.

I moved to the mirror and practiced my speech a few more times. I practiced handing the big trophy to the mayor. Then I practiced smiling into the TV camera.

I yawned. Enough practice, I decided. I've got it down. I'm ready to go.

Piece of cake, I told myself.

You'll be awesome tomorrow, Max. You'll be a star.

How could I know I was hours away from the biggest *disaster* of my life?

3

THE NEXT MORNING, I stepped into the new Jefferson Elementary Natatorium (that's a fancy word for indoor swimming pool). I had my fingers crossed. *Please,* I thought. *Please,* don't let me drop the trophy on my foot or something.

The huge new building was painted in cheerful blues and yellows and had a cool roof that we could slide open on sunny days! Like today. A beautiful, warm day.

Sunlight glimmered on the pool water in bright patches of gold light. I took a deep breath. I love that chlorine smell!

All the Jefferson students were packed tightly around three sides of the pool. Their voices echoed off the tile walls.

At one end, I saw a tall podium. The silver school trophy stood on a table beside it.

I started to feel even more nervous as I walked up to the podium. My mouth felt dry. And my heart started fluttering like a butterfly's wings.

Two TV workers were busy plugging in cables

and moving lights. Behind them, I saw our principal, Mrs. Wright, talking to Mayor Stank. They were laughing about something.

Mayor Stank is a short, chubby guy. He's shaped kinda like a turkey. He wore a tight gray suit with a gray vest. His bald head glowed like a lightbulb under the bright sunlight.

I walked closer. The mayor's tiny black eyes squinted over a chubby, round nose. His thin black mustache—two little lines—twitched as he talked. Beads of sweat clung to his forehead.

I hung back. But Mrs. Wright greeted me and pulled me over to the mayor. "Mayor Stank, this is Max Doyle," she said. "Max was chosen to present the trophy because he's at the top of his class."

Mayor Stank shook hands with me. His hand was soft and sweaty. "Congratulations, Max," he said.

He stared at the swollen bulge that Colin had left on my forehead. "I see you have a very big head," he said. "Lots of room for brains!" He erupted in a booming laugh that echoed off the tiles.

I gritted my teeth. Nice work, Colin, I thought.

Mrs. Wright stepped up to the podium. She waved her hands to signal for everyone to quiet down. The TV camera was pointed at her. She gave the mayor a welcoming speech. And she talked about how wonderful the new natatorium was.

Then Mayor Stank stepped up to the podium. He gave a speech too. As he talked, his big belly bobbed up and down inside the tight suit. And sweat rolled down his bald head.

I didn't hear a word he said. I was busy practicing *my* speech. I repeated it in my head, over and over.

And then I heard applause. Mrs. Wright gave me a little shove. "Go, Max."

My turn!

I took a deep breath and stepped up beside the mayor. I cleared my throat and prepared to give my talk.

And that's when I saw the two ghosts pop up at my sides.

"What are you *doing* here?" I cried.

4

I HAD BEGGED THEM not to come. But here they were, grinning at me.

They haunt me. Wherever I go.

Their names are Nicky and Tara Roland. Nicky is my age—eleven. Tara is nine. They appeared in my room one night. They said they used to live in my house.

I'm the only one who can see and hear them. Lucky me, right?

At first, I was scared. I mean, who wants ghosts popping in and out of your room? But then I started to feel sorry for them.

Nicky was a nice kid, but very sad. He didn't know how he and his sister had died. He didn't know how they became ghosts.

Tara was cute but a little bossy, a little spoiled. But she was sad too. She missed her mom and dad. She *hated* being a ghost.

Soon we became friends.

We made a deal. I'd help Nicky and Tara find their parents. And they would help me become a cooler guy. They promised to help me show my dad that I'm not a worthless wimp.

Good deal, right?

Well, I *did* help them find their parents. It wasn't easy. We had to fight an evil ghost named Phears, who was out to capture Nicky and Tara.

We managed to destroy Phears and find Mr. and Mrs. Roland. But guess what? Nicky and Tara are still living with me. Their parents are ghosts too. They went off to find a way to bring the family back to life.

We don't know when they will return. It might be months. It might be years.

So you see, I've kept my side of the bargain. I've helped them a lot.

But every time they try to help me, something goes wrong. And I end up looking like a total jerk.

But please—not today. Not *today*!

I stared at them. They both are tall and thin. Nicky's dark hair is short, and spiked up in front. Tara wore a floppy red hat, and dangling red plastic earrings to match.

"What are you doing here?" I asked again. "I begged you to stay away today."

Of course, I was the only one in the whole natatorium who could see or hear them.

Nicky slapped me on the back. "We came to help you out," he said.

"Don't be nervous, Max," Tara said. "Just because the whole school is watching and thousands more people are staring at you on TV."

"You're *making* me nervous!" I said.

Mayor Stank turned around. "Sorry, Max. Is there a problem?"

"Go ahead, Maxie," Tara said. "Give him your speech."

"Just shut up!" I told her.

Mayor Stank's mouth dropped open. "*What* did you say to me, young man?"

"Max, you're keeping the mayor waiting," Nicky said. "Want *me* to give your speech?"

"Shut up," I said. "I mean it."

Mayor Stank's face turned bright red. "You're telling me to shut up?"

"I wasn't talking to you," I said.

My voice went out over the loudspeaker. Everyone laughed and hooted. The laughter bounced off the tile walls.

I grabbed for the trophy. But Tara picked it up first.

The audience gasped. It looked as if the trophy was floating in midair.

"Um, my new magic trick!" I said into the microphone. "The Floating Trophy trick."

"Calm down, Max," Tara said. "Nicky and I are just trying to help you."

"Max's hands are shaking," Nicky said. "Tara, *you* give the mayor the trophy."

"I'm warning you—*go away!*" I shouted.

"Go away? You're telling me to go away?" the mayor shouted angrily. "Young man, you are very *rude!*"

"S-sorry," I stammered.

I knew I couldn't explain. So I leaned into the microphone and tried to start my speech. "Mayor Stank, thank you for helping us all make a real *splash* . . ."

Tara held on to the big silver trophy. I made a grab for it. "Give it to me!"

"No, I want to give it to the mayor!"

I *told* you she was bossy.

She grabbed it back.

It must have looked pretty funny as Tara and I had a tug-of-war with the trophy. Wild hoots and laughter rang out all around.

Finally, I swung it away from her.

But the trophy flew out of my hands.

It made a deafening *clonk* as it smacked the mayor in the head.

He groaned and toppled backward. His arms sailed up in the air as he did a backward flop into the pool. *Smack!*

What a splash!

"Oh noooo," I groaned as Mayor Stank sank under the water.

He dropped all the way to the bottom. Then his bald head bobbed above the surface. He began kicking and slapping the water like a wild man.

"I can't swim!" he screamed. "Help me! *I can't swim!*"

5

I STARED IN HORROR from the edge of the pool. Mayor Stank's head disappeared below the surface. A few seconds later, he bobbed back up, choking and sputtering.

"Help me! I can't swim!"

"Go save him, Max!" Tara gave me a hard shove.

"I—I don't know how to rescue anyone," I stammered. "I was absent that day in lifesaving class."

I saw several teachers leap into the water. Then a lot of splashing and shouting.

"Be a hero, Max," Nicky said. "Go—quick!"

My heart pounding, I stared at the mayor. He was bouncing on the water like a crazed porpoise. He was kicking and slapping and sputtering. The teachers struggled to grab him.

He floated close to the side of the pool. His head went down again.

"Get him, Max!" Tara cried.

I bent over the side. Made a grab for his feet. Missed.

I grabbed again. This time, I wrapped my hands around the legs of his suit pants.

"Got him!" I cried.

I pulled hard. Leaning back, I gave a hard tug—

—and pulled off the mayor's pants!

"Whoa!" I staggered back against the wall. I had the mayor's pants in my hands.

Finally, the teachers pulled the mayor out of the water. He stood on the side of the pool in his underwear, shivering and shaking the water from his body.

A teacher came running with some towels. Mayor Stank wrapped a towel around his hips to cover his bare legs. Then he used another towel to mop his bald head.

He squinted at me angrily. He glared at the pair of gray pants in my hands. He scowled and shook a fist at me.

Mrs. Wright hurried over. "Max, I—I'm speechless," she said. "I am very, very angry. Can you explain what just happened here?"

I handed the soggy pants to her. "Would you believe it was an accident?" I said.

Mrs. Wright squeezed my shoulder. "See me in my office after school," she said through gritted teeth. "Don't plan on going anywhere, Max. You and I are going to have a long, long talk."

Tara appeared at my side. "Want Nicky and me to come with you?" she asked.

6

I **DIDN'T GET HOME** till almost dinnertime. Mrs.
Wright and I had a very long talk. Only, she did all
the talking.

Nicky and Tara were waiting for me in my
room when I got home. "Sorry, Max," Tara said,
putting a hand on my shoulder. "Guess that didn't
go very well."

"I really wanted to hear your speech," Nicky
said.

"What a shame the mayor ruined everything,"
Tara added.

I let out a scream. "The *mayor* ruined everything?" I screamed again. "You got that wrong.
You two ruined everything!"

I'd never felt so angry in my life.

Tara shrank back against the window. "We
were only trying to help," she said. "Why didn't
you let me give him the trophy? I told you I really
wanted to."

"You can't do everything you want!" I

shouted. "You ruined *everything*. You're ruining my whole *life*!"

Her mouth dropped open. "You're hurting my feelings, Max."

"We were only trying to help," Nicky said. "Remember? We promised to help each other?"

I tossed my backpack at him. It went right through him and bounced off the wall.

"Don't be angry," Tara said.

"Angry?" I cried. "Angry? I'm *furious*!"

"Max, think how dull your life would be without us," Nicky said.

"I *like* dull!" I screamed. "After living with you, I want a dull life. *Years* and *years* of dull! I hope *nothing* interesting ever happens to me again! I want you to go away. Go *away*!"

Tara gasped. Nicky backed against the wall. They both vanished.

My brother, Colin, peered into my room. "What are you doing, Fat Face? Why are you screaming like a baby? Need your bottle?"

"These are screaming exercises," I said. "It's a new workout. To build my lung power."

Colin stepped into my room. I saw that he was wearing boxing gloves. "You can help me with *my* new workout," he said. He raised his gloves. "Come on, punk. Let's box."

I backed away. "No. No thanks," I said. "Sounds like a lot of fun. But no thanks."

Colin danced closer. He waved the gloves in my face. "Help me with my boxing workout."

"But . . . I don't have any gloves!" I said.

"You don't need any," Colin replied. "You're the punching bag."

Powpow powpow pow powpow pow.

7

COLIN WAS HAVING an outstanding workout. Who says I'm not a good athlete? I make a *great* punching bag.

Finally, after about ten thousand punches, Mom shouted for us to come downstairs to dinner.

"Thanks for the workout," Colin said.

I was holding my stomach, in too much pain to answer. I stumbled down to the kitchen.

Unless we have company, we eat dinner at the kitchen table with the TV on. Dad likes to watch the Channel 600 news because they show all the car accidents in town.

Dad loves to watch car accidents. Maybe it's because he's a big Mack truck of a guy who can mow anyone down. My dad is huge and red-faced, with a shiny head that's almost totally bald except for a strip of short bristly hair that curves around from ear to ear. He has a bright red and blue tattoo of a fire-breathing dragon on one bicep.

My mom and dad look really funny when they

stand together. He's so big and wide, and she's tiny and short and skitters around like a little bird.

"Steak. My fave," I said. I leaned over my plate and took a deep sniff. "Mmmmm."

"A special dinner tonight, Max," Mom said. "Since you had a special day. And your dad has a special announcement to make. How did it go at school this morning? Did the mayor like your speech?"

"Uh . . . yeah," I muttered.

"Wow. That car totally blew up!" Dad said. He already had steak sauce all over his cheeks and chin. "Did you see that head-on crash? Whoa, boy! Show that one again!"

He always talks to the TV while we eat.

"Maxie, would you like mashed potatoes?" Mom asked.

"Maxie likes soft food," Colin said. "Because he's a baby."

"Colin, don't call your brother names on his special day," Mom scolded.

"I wasn't," Colin said.

Dad gulped down a huge chunk of steak. Still swallowing, he pointed to me with his fork. "Max, you were there when it happened. I heard some jerky kid at your school knocked the mayor into the new swimming pool."

Gulp.

I decided to play innocent. "Really?" I said.

"And then the kid de-pantsed the mayor! Hee-hee-hee. He pulled Stank's pants off in front of everyone!" Dad started laughing and choking at the same time. Mom had to walk over and slap him on the back.

"Isn't that a riot?" Dad pounded the table with one hand. "Can you believe a stupid kid did that to the mayor?"

"I . . . can't believe it," I mumbled. I hid my face behind my pile of potatoes.

"Hey, check it out!" Colin cried. He pointed to the TV. "It's on the news. The thing at your school. Watch!"

I couldn't breathe. My heart sank to my knees. I wanted to dive headfirst into the mashed potatoes and not come out.

All four of us watched me on TV as I swung the trophy, clonked Mayor Stank in the head, and sent him flying into the pool. And then, a few seconds later, there I was, leaning over the edge of the pool, yanking off the big man's trousers.

Must See TV.

It took a while. But Mom finally recognized me. She pressed her hands to her face. "Oh no. Oh no. It was *you,* Max."

"You stupid klutz!" Colin cried. He tossed a dinner roll across the table. It bounced off my forehead. "Max, now the *whole city* knows what a total jerk you are! How could you do it?"

"I had help," I muttered.

Dad turned away from the TV. He wiped the steak sauce from his face with his T-shirt sleeve. He was staring hard at me the whole time.

"You're a disgrace, Max," he said. "It's a good thing we're moving away."

My heart skipped a beat. I let out a loud, startled gasp. "Huh? Moving?"

Dad nodded. "Yeah. That's my special announcement. I got a job in Dallas. We're selling this house and moving to Texas."

8

MOM SMILED AT COLIN and me. "That's why we're having this lovely steak dinner. To celebrate the good news."

Good news?

Was it good news?

Leave my friends? My school?

Start over again in a whole new place?

That's not good news. That's *bad* news.

But whoa. Wait. Hold on a minute.

No more ghosts! I could get away from those ghosts. Have a normal life.

Goodbye, Nicky and Tara. Goodbye, pests! I'm off to Texas and leaving you behind.

No way could they ruin my life in Texas!

Colin turned to Dad. Another car crash came on the TV news. Colin had to shake Dad by the shoulders to get his attention. "You know I've got to work out, Dad. Keep my body fit. Will there be room in the new house for my own gym?"

Dad nodded. "Yeah. Plenty of room. Wow.

That guy got rear-ended by three SUVs. His car looks like an accordion!"

Colin grinned at me. "My own gym. Max, I won't have to use you as a punching bag anymore." His grin grew wider. "Well . . . only sometimes."

I wasn't thinking about Colin's gym. I was thinking about my new life. A life without ghosts. A life where I wouldn't be embarrassed in front of the whole town!

The car accident report was over. Dad turned to me. "Texas will make a man out of you, Max," he said. "You'll learn to ride horses."

"Horses?" I said. My voice cracked. "Horses make me sneeze. Even when I see them on TV!"

"You'll get used to them," Mom said softly. "Let's all have a lovely celebration dinner. Enjoy your steak, Maxie."

"Hey—who let Buster in the house?" Dad shouted.

I didn't see the big dog in time. All I saw was a blur of dark fur.

Buster leaped up and grabbed the whole steak off my plate. He gobbled it down in seconds without even chewing.

"My steak!" I cried. I stared down at the dog, who was licking his chops.

Dad tossed back his head and hee-hawed. "That dog is *crazy* for meat!"

I gazed at my empty plate. My stomach growled. Or was that Buster?

Mom turned to my brother. "Colin, share your steak with Max," she said.

"I can't," Colin said. "Coach says I need protein." He sawed off a big chunk of meat, shoved it into his mouth, and chewed it in my face.

Mom let out a sigh. "Sorry, Max. There's no more steak." She stood up and walked to the food cabinet. She brought me a bowl and the box of Frosted Flakes. "Here. You like these."

So I ate Frosted Flakes while everyone else ate steak.

"I've already put the house on the market," Dad said. "Mr. Grimmus, my new boss, is coming all the way from Texas in a few days. He wants to meet you all. I guess he wants to check us out. Make sure I'm right for the job."

Mom patted Dad's hand. "Of course you're right for the job," she said.

Dad let out a really loud burp.

Sometimes he and Colin have burping contests. They go for loudness and for length of time. I tried to join in once, but I barfed up my entire dinner.

We all turned back to the TV. On the news, they were showing the swimming pool accident again. There I was, holding up the mayor's pants while he flopped and floundered in the pool.

Dad shook his head. "It's a really good thing we're leaving town," he said. "I've met Mayor Stank. He's not a nice man. Believe me. He holds a grudge."

A chill gripped the back of my neck. *A grudge?*

I climbed the stairs to my room. I felt strange—excited and worried at the same time. I decided to practice my magic. That always calms me down.

I picked up the milk bottles I'd been working with. I'm trying to teach myself to juggle full milk bottles. I think that will be a really exciting finish to my act.

If I drop one, the bottle will shatter and milk will fly all over. It will be messy. But I don't plan to drop any.

I started practicing with just two bottles. They were heavy and hard to toss and catch.

"How can you juggle at a time like this?" a voice said. Tara appeared beside me. She grabbed one of the bottles. "We heard everything, Max."

Nicky appeared in front of me. "You're moving! What are we going to do?" he asked.

I shrugged. "Beats me."

"You can't move. You *can't*!" Tara cried. She was tossing a milk bottle from hand to hand. I took it away from her.

"We have to wait in this house for Mom and

Dad to come back," Nicky said, pacing back and forth. "Tara and I can't leave."

"You'll be safe here," I said. "It won't be so bad. Someone else will move in and help you. You'll be okay."

"But we *need* you, Max," Tara said. "You're the only one who can see and hear us."

"You have to stop your dad," Nicky said. "You can't let him move your family away."

"What can I do?" I said. "I can't stop him. We're moving as soon as he sells the house."

Nicky and Tara grew silent. I could see they were thinking hard.

"Hey, you wouldn't try anything—would you?" I asked. "You wouldn't try to stop us from moving!"

Tara smiled at me. "Of course not, Maxie."

9

ON SATURDAY AFTERNOON, I walked to Aaron's house to tell him the bad news. Aaron and I have been friends since we were little kids.

Even when he was a baby, he was kinda strange. For example, he learned to walk—and then a few months later, he learned to crawl.

I knew he'd be upset about my family moving away. It was going to be really tough for both of us. For one thing, Aaron had the first season of *Buffy,* and I had the second season. How would we ever trade episodes?

Aaron greeted me at the door and led me to his room. He was wearing a blue and red *Star Trek* cap, sideways; brown shorts; and a T-shirt that said: DON'T WEAR THIS.

Where does he find these dumb shirts?

He closed the door behind us. "Shhh." He put a finger to his lips. "I brought home a jar of honey."

I squinted at him. "Honey? Why?"

"I'm going to pour it into my sister's bed," he whispered.

"Why?" I asked.

"Revenge," he said.

Aaron spends a big part of every day getting revenge on his six-year-old sister, Kaytlin.

Aaron giggled. "Tonight she'll climb into bed. She won't see the honey till it's too late. She'll be sticky for the rest of her life." He giggled some more.

"I came over to tell you something," I said.

"Shhh. Not now," he whispered. "I'll show you the jar of honey." He grabbed his backpack and pulled it open.

His mouth dropped open and his eyes bulged. He let out a groan. "Oh noooo."

I peered into the backpack. The lid had come off the jar. The thick, sticky honey had spilled all over Aaron's books and binders.

He lifted his math book out. It was dripping with a heavy layer of gunk.

"Ruined," Aaron moaned. "I'm ruined." He dropped the soaked textbook into the backpack. "Kaytlin did this!" he cried, shaking a fist. "She did this. This means *war*!"

"But Aaron, I need to tell you something," I said.

He tossed the backpack down and flew out the door. I followed him to the kitchen.

"Maybe we have some in this cabinet," he said. He pulled open the door and began shoving jars and bottles out of his way. "Yes! Here it is!" He held up a jar. "A big jar. We haven't lost. This war is just beginning."

"*We?*"

He pulled off the lid and tossed it aside. Then he ran past me with the jar raised in front of him. His eyes were wild. His mouth was twisted in an evil grin.

I followed him down the long hall. He stopped at his sister's room and peeked in. "She's not home," he said. "Come on. Let's rock and roll."

He tiptoed to Kaytlin's dresser and slid open the top drawer He giggled. "It's her underwear drawer. Check it out."

I didn't really want to see Kaytlin's underwear. But I didn't have a choice. I peeked into the drawer.

Her underpants were neatly folded in rows, organized by color.

"Aaron, I really have to tell you something," I tried again.

But he motioned for me to hush. Then he leaned the honey jar against the drawer and tipped it upside down. Slowly, slowly, the thick goop started to pour out onto Kaytlin's underpants.

Aaron moved the jar slowly back and forth. He had covered two rows of underpants when his mother stepped into the room.

"Aaron? What on earth are you doing?" she asked.

Aaron turned around, still holding the jar over the drawer. "Uh . . . nothing," he said.

"You are going to be doing nothing for a long, long time," she said. "Because you are grounded for life."

"Not again," Aaron said.

So I had to leave. I didn't have a chance to tell Aaron my sad news. I decided to e-mail him when I got home.

10

THE SUN HAD GONE DOWN. I started to walk home from Aaron's house. Fog floated in, making the trees and houses hazy.

I heard soft thuds behind me. I realized that someone was following me. *Again!*

I turned. I saw him. The boy dressed in black. The boy with the old man's face.

My heart started to pound. My legs felt shaky and weak. I decided to stop and face him. "Who are you?" I cried. "What do you want?"

And then once again, he whispered the words: *"I'm watching . . . I'm watching . . ."*

Huh? Watching? Watching *me*?

Why?

His voice sent a shiver down my back.

Suddenly, car headlights swept over the ground as an SUV turned the corner. The light poured right through the boy.

Right through him!

He took off, bending low to avoid the light.

And I realized he was a ghost. He had to be a ghost.

I took a deep breath. No sign of him now. The light had frightened him away. I turned and ran home.

I found Mom in the kitchen, wiping down the counter. "Mom, someone followed me!" I cried.

"That's nice, dear," she said. She didn't look up. She was busy cleaning.

"No, Mom—listen!" I cried. "It was scary. A boy—he chased me. He had an old man's face. I—"

Finally, she turned around. "Oh my goodness!" she cried. "Look at you. Max, this won't do! The Marvins will be here any minute."

"Who?"

"Get clean. Get changed. Clean your room. Clean, clean, clean!" she cried.

I stared at her. "I don't understand. A strange old man chased me. I think he might have been a ghost—"

"No time for your ghost stories," Mom said. She started to push me out of the kitchen. "Mrs. Flake will be here soon. She's the real estate agent, Maxie."

"Mrs. Flake?"

"Don't laugh at her name, whatever you do," Mom warned. "She doesn't know it's a funny name."

"But Mom—" I started.

"She's bringing a nice young couple. The Marvins. To look at our house."

No way would Mom listen to my story. With a sigh, I heaved myself upstairs. I pulled off my clothes and carried them to the laundry room.

I took a hot shower. Put on a fresh pair of jeans and a T-shirt.

"Clean, clean, clean," Mom had said. So I did my best to straighten my room. I made my bed and I picked up a lot of junk from the floor and shoved it into my closet.

I felt really tense. I couldn't stop thinking about that guy in black.

I needed to talk to somebody. "Nicky? Tara? Where are you?" I called.

No answer.

Where were they? Were they angry at me because I wanted to move and leave them behind? They'd been disappearing a lot lately. They said they couldn't control it.

I needed to talk to them. I needed to tell them I knew they were angry at me. But they had to understand—there was nothing I could do about it.

I picked up three of my six heavy milk bottles and started to juggle them. I knew the juggling would calm me down. But I was so tense, I couldn't get my rhythm going.

When the front doorbell rang, all three bottles flew from my hands.

With a wild swipe, I grabbed them all before they hit the floor. Mom wouldn't be too happy to find broken glass and pools of milk all over the rug.

I heard voices downstairs. A woman said, "What a charming place." Then a man said, "This is just the right size."

I set the milk bottles on my desk. I lined up all six to make them look neat.

A few minutes later, Mom led everyone into my bedroom. Mrs. Flake was a white-haired woman with flashing blue eyes and bright purple lipstick. The Marvins were blond and thin and nice-looking.

Mr. Marvin wore a red tie and a blue blazer. His wife wore a short denim skirt and a yellow T-shirt.

"This is Max," Mom said. I nodded to them. "You'll have to excuse the messiness," Mom said.

Messiness? I cleaned everything up!

Mrs. Marvin gave me a sweet smile. "How old are you, Max?" she asked. I hate when grown-ups ask that question.

"Eleven years, eleven months, and four days," I said.

They all laughed. "Max likes math," Mom said.

Mrs. Flake waved a hand around the room.

"Notice the windows," she told the Marvins. "They give a lot of light."

The Marvins walked around my room. "Very charming," Mrs. Marvin said. "What are those?"

She walked up to the row of milk bottles. Her husband followed her.

"Do you collect old milk bottles?" he asked.

"No. I juggle," I said.

"You juggle bottles filled with milk?" Mrs. Flake asked.

I didn't have a chance to answer. The six bottles suddenly floated up into the air. And then, with a loud *pop pop pop*, the lids flew off.

Nicky and Tara! They *had* to be doing this!

I knew it. They're angry—and they're trying to chase the Marvins away! They think they can stop me from moving!

I let out a cry as gushers of milk flew up high—almost to the ceiling—then came pouring down over the Marvins.

They both ducked, but they weren't fast enough. The milk plopped onto their heads, their shoulders, their clothes. Thick white clots clung to their hair.

"It's *sour*!" Mrs. Marvin cried, her hands in her hair. "Oh, it smells. It *smells*!"

I held my nose. But I could still smell the putrid odor of the sour milk.

Mrs. Flake was gagging and choking. Holding

42

her hands over her face, she staggered out into the hall.

The Marvins flapped their arms and shook their bodies. They were drenched in the thick, sour glop.

Wiping clots of milk from their eyes, moaning and choking, they staggered after Mrs. Flake.

A few seconds later, the front door slammed. The Marvins were gone.

Mom glared angrily at me, hands on her hips. She tapped one shoe on the floor. I could see she was too angry to speak.

I took my fingers off my nose. "Mom," I said, "does this mean they won't buy the house?"

11

MOM AND I WORKED for more than an hour to clean up the mess. She kept biting her bottom lip and shaking her head. She didn't say a word to me the whole time.

She wore a scarf over her nose and mouth to keep out the smell. We both had buckets and sponges. The milk had soaked the wall, the floor, my desk—everywhere. I pulled big clots of it from my computer keyboard.

Mom didn't talk. But Dad had a lot to say when he got home.

"Max, you're part of this family. You can't pull stupid stunts like this to keep us from moving."

Of course, Jerk Face Colin had to chime in: "There's sour milk left in one bottle. Make Max drink it, Dad. Make him drink it!"

For once, Dad ignored Colin. "You're lucky, Max," he said. "The Marvins called. They took very long showers, and the smell has almost come off them. They're still interested in the house."

44

Dad shook his huge fist at me. "I'm warning you—no more magic tricks or funny business."

I could have explained that the sour milk explosion wasn't my fault. But whenever I tried to tell Mom and Dad about Nicky and Tara, they laughed. They said I was too old to have imaginary friends.

After dinner, I rushed to my room to have a good long talk with those two ghosts. I nearly choked when I stepped inside. How long would my room smell like puke?

"Nicky? Tara? Where are you? Are you hiding?" I called, gazing around my bedroom. "How could you *do* that to me? You got me into *major* trouble."

My hands were balled into tight fists. I felt ready to explode. I wanted to let them know how angry I was.

But . . . no sign of them.

Then I felt a whoosh of cold air. And there they were, perched on the edge of my bed.

"We're back!" Tara said. She smiled at me. "Wish we could control all this coming and going."

"We keep vanishing and we can't help it," Nicky said.

I glared angrily at them. "Give me a break. You were here the whole time."

Tara sniffed the air. Nicky sniffed too. "Puke!" he cried. "Did some animal *die* in here?"

45

"Ohhh—sick! Your room smells *sick*!" Tara said, covering her nose.

I stood with my hands on my waist. "Guys, don't act innocent," I said. "I know you made the bottles explode. Now my parents are *furious* at me. And it's all your fault."

Tara jumped up. She grabbed my arm. "Maxie, it *can't* be our fault. We haven't been here since this morning."

"Oh, sure," I said angrily. "I guess the milk bottles all popped open by themselves."

Nicky squinted at me. "Milk bottles?" He sniffed again. "Oh, yuck. Is that sour milk?"

I jerked my arm away from Tara. She backed up, surprised.

"You got me into *major* trouble again!" I shouted. "Now do you understand why I can't *wait* to move to Texas?"

"But we really didn't do anything, dude," Nicky said.

"No way. We weren't here," Tara said.

They both raised their right hands. "We swear."

"Then who did it?" I screamed.

Colin burst into my room. He glanced around. Of course, he couldn't see Nicky and Tara standing right in front of him. "Hey, loser, who are you yelling at?"

I swallowed. "Uh . . . myself," I said. "I'm yelling at myself for letting those bottles explode."

Colin sniffed. "Smells like puke," he said. "Know what? That smell will seep into your skin tonight while you sleep. At school, your new name will be the Human Puke."

"Go away, Colin," I pleaded. "I want to yell at myself some more. I really deserve it."

He grinned. "Yes, you do." He sniffed the air a few times, made a disgusted face, and hurried out.

I turned back to my two ghost friends.

"You believe us, don't you, Max?" Nicky said. "You believe we didn't make the bottles pop open?"

I stared from one to the other. "If you two didn't do it," I said, "who did?"

Nicky and Tara both shrugged.

I suddenly felt a little frightened. Were they telling the truth? If they were . . . who had made the milk bottles explode?

Had someone else been in my room? Another ghost?

The boy in black? Again, I pictured him. His face changing from young to old. The car headlights piercing right through him . . .

"I'm watching . . . ," he had whispered. *"I'm watching . . ."*

Had he been here in my room? Did he make the bottles explode? Was another ghost out to get me?

12

I CHANGED FOR BED, but I couldn't sleep. For one thing, I couldn't get the puke smell out of my nose.

And I had a tingling feeling. My skin prickled.

I had a hunch. A frightening hunch.

I climbed out of bed and crept to the window. I pushed aside the curtains and squinted down to the front yard.

And yes. There he was.

"Oh no!" I uttered a hoarse cry.

I stared down at the figure in black. He stood half hidden in darkness beside the big birch tree near the driveway.

I couldn't see his face. But I saw his frail, thin body huddled against the tree trunk.

And then the moonlight shifted through the fluttering branches. Light washed over him.

I saw him clearly.

I saw his face. *A young boy's face.*

Leaning out the open window, I saw dark eyes peering up at me. Short dark hair. A long slender face, silvery in the bright moonlight.

I gripped the windowsill.

I froze in fright.

And as I stared down into the patch of moon-light, the boy's face changed. It grew longer. It stretched. His eyes pulled back. His snout slid forward.

Dark fur sprouted over his head. His hair stood on end.

Gripped with horror, I stood frozen at the window. Staring out . . . *at the face of a growling wolf*!

"Noooo . . ." A whispered moan escaped my throat.

The wind swirled into my open window, fluttering my pajamas.

The wolf snarled and floated off the ground. A boy in black with a wolf face, eyes glowing red, jagged teeth snapping . . .

He floated up, rising toward my window.

"No!" I screamed. "No—please!"

I slammed the window shut. I pulled the shade down.

I backed away, trembling. "Don't come in. Please—don't come in."

Silence now.

The wind rattled the windowpane, as if trying to burst through.

Just the wind now.

No wolf boy shooting through the glass into my room.

Another ghost. Another creature come to haunt me.

No wonder I wanted to move away from all this. No wonder.

Did I sleep at all that night?

Three guesses.

13

MONDAY MORNING I made a new friend.

I was walking across the playground at school, searching for Aaron. I still wanted to tell him the news that my family was moving to Texas. And I wanted to tell him about the boy in black, the ghost boy who could change his face.

I *had* to tell someone. I was really frightened.

A bunch of fourth graders were having a soccer match on the field. Boys against girls. Not a very good game. A lot of laughing and bumping into each other and knocking each other down.

I watched for a few moments, but of course I didn't see Aaron.

Aaron would *never* play soccer. He never runs. He worries that if he ever ran really fast, his feet might leave the ground and he'd fly up to the sun.

I told you Aaron is weird.

When I turned back toward school, a kid I'd never seen before came hurrying up to me.

"Are you Max?" he asked.

I nodded. "Yeah."

He had straight blond hair that fell over a wide forehead, and shiny blue eyes. He had dimples in both cheeks when he smiled. He wore a navy blue sweatshirt over baggy khaki cargo pants, torn at one knee.

He tugged back a strand of blond hair. "I'm the new kid in school," he said. "Quentin Jones." His eyes were so round and blue, they looked like they were made of glass.

"How's it going?" I asked.

He shrugged. "I don't like being the new kid."

That made me think about *me* moving to a new school. In a few months, *I'd* be the new kid.

I looked over his shoulder, hoping to see Aaron. "What grade are you in?" I asked.

"Sixth. Like you," Quentin said.

How did he know so much about me?

"Cool," I said.

"I hear you're into magic," Quentin said. "So am I."

"Who told you I'm into magic?" I asked.

He brushed back his hair again. "Ms. McDonald," he said. "She said I should talk to you because we both do magic tricks."

Wow. I couldn't believe another kid was into magic. Everyone else in school thought I was weird.

Quentin reached into his pocket. "Pick a card," he said. He held a deck of cards out to me.

I picked one. The three of clubs.

Quentin took the card and didn't look at it. He slid it back into the deck. Then he shuffled the deck three times.

He handed the stack to me. "Go ahead, Max. Find your card."

I turned the deck face up and quickly sorted through the cards. "Hey, my card isn't in here," I said.

Quentin flashed me his dimpled smile. "I know," he said.

I searched through the deck again.

"Check your pants pocket," Quentin said, pointing.

I reached into my pants pocket—and pulled out the three of clubs.

"That's *outstanding*!" I told him. "How did you do that?"

His smile grew wider. The clear blue eyes flashed. "You like that one?"

"Yeah," I said. "Could you teach it to me?"

He nodded. "Maybe I could come over to your house sometime and we could teach each other some new tricks."

"Excellent!" I said. I stared at the three of clubs in my hand. "Yeah. We'll teach each other," I said. "Excellent!"

Quentin's eyes flashed again. "I have some tricks you won't believe," he said.

14

I BURST INTO THE KITCHEN after school. "Mom, can I invite a new friend over to practice magic tricks?"

"Not today," she said. "We have people coming over."

I sniffed the air. "Wow. What smells so awesome?"

"I'm baking a pie," Mom said, turning from the oven. "A lemon meringue pie."

"Mmmm. For dinner?" I said, tossing my backpack onto the kitchen counter. I checked through the pile of mail by the phone. My new *Fear Factor* Fan Club newsletter had arrived.

"No, it's for the Marvins," Mom said. She moved to the sink and started to wash out some pans. "Mrs. Flake is bringing them back to look at the house again. I thought I'd bake a little dessert."

"They're coming back?" I asked.

"Yes. They'll be here any minute. So pick up that backpack. Take it upstairs. Make sure your room is clean, Max. I don't want any funny business this time."

"For sure," I muttered.

I dragged my backpack up the stairs to my room and tossed it into the closet. "Nicky? Tara? Are you up here?" I called.

No answer.

Where were they?

It was silent upstairs. No music pounding from Colin's room. He probably had track team practice at school.

"If you're here," I called to the ghosts, "no tricks. I'm warning you. I don't want to get in trouble again."

I straightened my desk. Made a neat pile of my *Star Trek* and *Lord of the Rings* magazines on my bookshelf. Hid some magic equipment in the closet. Shoved a pile of dirty clothes under the bed.

There. The room looked pretty good.

I sat down on the edge of the bed with a sigh. I liked my room. I didn't want to leave it. And I'd finally made a new friend, a guy who also was into magic.

But I knew my life had to be better in Texas— no ghosts constantly embarrassing me, no creepy wolf boys floating after me, terrifying me.

I heard the doorbell ring downstairs. "No funny business!" Mom shouted up. "Promise?"

She didn't wait for my answer. She pulled open

the front door, and I heard her greeting Mrs. Flake and the Marvins.

Soon they were inspecting the house again. I sat on the edge of my bed, waiting for them.

When they reached my room, they all stopped in my doorway and peeked around. "No more milk bottles?" Mrs. Marvin asked.

I shook my head. "No. Sorry about that," I said. "I put all my magic stuff away."

"Magic is a nice hobby," Mrs. Flake said, stepping into the room. "How did you get into it, Matt?"

"My name is Max," I said. "I don't know. I just liked it."

The Marvins stayed in the doorway. I think they were afraid to enter my room. "The room is a little small," Mr. Marvin said. "Maybe we could tear that wall down and combine the two bedrooms."

They moved to Colin's bedroom. They spent a lot of time looking at the rest of the house. They kept talking about moving doors and tearing things down.

When they were finished, I followed them to the kitchen. They all sat with my mom around our kitchen table. "Max, bring over the lemon meringue pie so I can slice it," Mom said.

"You shouldn't have baked a pie," Mrs. Marvin said. "That was so nice of you."

"Lemon meringue pie is my favorite," Mr. Marvin said.

I picked up the pie in both hands and started to carry it to the table.

"Whoa—!"

I let out a startled cry as the pie flew out of my hands. I made a wild grab for it. But it floated out of my reach—and across the room.

It picked up speed as it shot toward the kitchen table.

I gasped as the pie rose up high, turned upside down—and plopped down hard on Mr. Marvin's head.

It made a sick *sploosh* sound. No one moved for a moment. Gobs of meringue and yellow custard goop oozed down Mr. Marvin's face.

He jumped to his feet, sputtering. He wiped lemon custard from his eyes.

"You—you brat!" Mrs. Flake shouted at me. "You *threw* that pie!"

"No!" I protested. I waved my hands. "No way. I didn't—"

But no one was listening to me. The Marvins were on their feet now. Mom handed Mr. Marvin a dish towel, and he wiped big, gooey clumps of pie off his head.

"It was an accident!" Mom cried. She turned to me. "Right, Max?"

"Yeah. An accident," I said. "I tripped and—"

The Marvins stomped out of the kitchen. Mrs. Flake led the way to the front door. Everyone was talking at once.

Mrs. Flake said, "That boy should be locked up."

"He's crazy!" Mrs. Marvin agreed.

"Lemon meringue pie is *not* my favorite anymore," Mr. Marvin said.

The door slammed behind them.

Mom stood in the kitchen doorway, hands on her waist. She had her eyes shut tight, and she was tapping one foot on the floor. That's what she does when she's too angry to speak.

"I guess I'll be grounded in my room for the rest of my life," I said.

"You got that right," she said through clenched teeth.

I trudged up to my room. "Nicky? Tara? Where are you?" I demanded. "Why did you do that? Why did you get me into so much trouble?"

To my surprise, they appeared in front of my bed.

Tara blinked several times. "We're back," she said, tugging at her red hat.

"How long have we been gone?" Nicky asked, blinking, gazing around the room.

"Why did you drop that pie on Mr. Marvin?" I screamed. "I know you don't want the Marvins to buy the house. But you can't *do* that!"

Tara got this innocent look on her face. "Pie? We didn't drop any pie on anybody," she said.

"We've been gone," Nicky said. "We were asleep or something. You know. Off in Ghost Land. We just got back."

I rolled my eyes. "Shut up," I said. "Just shut up. I know what you're trying to do. You're trying to stop us from moving. But it won't work!"

"Sit down, Max," Nicky said. He guided me to the bed and pushed me onto it. "Sit down. Take a breath."

"We know who's been doing these things to the Marvins," Tara said. "It isn't us."

Nicky shook his head. His expression suddenly turned grim. "Max, you have other visitors," he said.

15

THE TWO GHOSTS SAT beside me on the edge of the bed. "We have bad news, Max," Tara said.

I swallowed. I thought about the boy in black with the face that kept changing. "*More* ghosts have come to haunt me?" I asked.

"Worse," Tara murmured. "Much worse."

"There are *ghouls* in the house," Nicky said. "Two of them."

"We saw them," Tara said. "I tried to take a photo of them with my cell phone, to show you. But my cell phone is dead."

"And ghouls don't show up in photos," Nicky added.

"Very helpful," I said.

Tara shrugged. "Well, I tried."

I took a deep breath. "Two ghouls? What are they doing here?" I cried. "What do they want? Why did they pick me?"

"Who knows?" Tara answered.

"They're being ghoulish," Nicky replied. "That's what ghouls do."

"But—but—how do we get rid of them?" I asked.

"We can't," Nicky said.

My heart skipped a beat. "Huh? We can't?"

"Well, *you* can't," Tara said. "It's too dangerous for you. Because you're alive. Living humans should not mess with ghouls."

"Tara and I will have to do the dirty job," Nicky said. "Maybe tonight." He shivered.

"Is it . . . dangerous?" I asked.

They both nodded.

"It won't be easy," Nicky said in a whisper.

"Let me show you something, Maxie," Tara said. She vanished for a moment. When she returned, she was holding a large book.

She handed it to me. It was very old and dusty. I couldn't read the title on the front. It had been smudged out.

I held it in both hands and flipped through the pages. They were yellowed and crumbling. The book smelled like a dusty old attic.

I handed it back to Tara. "What is it?" I brushed the dust off my hands.

"It's a book of ancient sorcery and magic spells," Tara said. "I found it in the basement of the big library downtown. Maybe I can find a spell to help us."

I stared at the old book. "Magic spells? For real?"

Tara dropped the book onto the bed and opened it. It had tiny type up and down the pages, and weird-looking drawings and diagrams.

"I've really gotten into these ancient spells," Tara said. "Mom and Dad went away to find something that will bring our family back to life. Well, maybe I can find a spell in this old book to help them."

"It's a mysterious book," Nicky said, flipping pages. "Tara has found all kinds of spells for bringing objects to life. But maybe there's one in here that can bring *humans* back to life!"

"But . . . but what about the ghouls?" I said. "Do you think you can find a magic spell to chase the ghouls away?"

Tara bit her bottom lip. "That's what I was hoping. . . ."

I gazed down at the crumbling old book. "You really think the spells in here work?"

"Of course," Tara said. "Why put them in a book if they don't work?" She turned a few pages. "Hey, I know. Let's try one!"

"Whoa. Hold on." Nicky backed away. "It could be dangerous, Tara."

She made a face at him. "Nicky, we're already *dead*. Remember? So how dangerous could it be?" She ran her finger down a column of tiny type.

Nicky tried to take the book from her. "Maybe you should study it more first."

Tara tugged it back. "You're such a worry-wart, Nicky. I'll do something simple. You don't have to be scared."

Nicky sighed. "That's what Mom always called me. A worrywart," he said softly. "I wish we knew when Mom and Dad were coming back. I sure miss them."

Tara wasn't listening. She was studying the spell book. "Here. I found one," she said. "Max, you can help me. Hold the book up while I recite the spell." She shoved it into my hands.

"Listen, guys," I said. "I know you two want to be alive again. But I'm not sure this spell thing is such a cool idea."

"No one asked you, Max," Tara said. "Just hold the book."

She dragged me over to my bookshelf. "What are these action figures?" She pointed.

"*Star Wars* characters," I said. "That's Darth Vader. That's C-3PO. They're very rare and very valuable."

"Watch. I'm going to bring them to life," Tara said.

"Are you *crazy*?" I cried. "I don't want Darth Vader walking around my room! He's totally *evil*—remember?"

"Max, don't worry," Nicky said. "It won't work. No way. Let Tara have her fun."

Tara punched Nicky hard in the chest. "Thanks for the support."

"Support? Oooh, big word for a little girl," Nicky said. He punched her in the arm.

She punched him in the stomach.

He punched her in the back. Then he grabbed her hat off her head and tossed it across my room.

"Uh . . . guys," I said. "Guys . . . ?"

Pushing back her hair, Tara turned to me. "Ignore him, Max. Once I master these spells, I'm going to bring *myself* back to life, and he can stay a ghost. Forever." She stuck her tongue out at her brother. Then she turned back to the action figures.

"Here. Just do C-3PO," I said. "He's harmless." I hid Darth Vader in the top drawer.

Tara bent over the book. "Hold it up higher. I can't see it."

I held the book higher. It was heavy. My arms started to ache. "Hope it's a short spell," I muttered.

"Shhh." Tara gave me a shove. "I have to concentrate."

"Concentrate on being a moron," Nicky said.

Tara glanced at him. "If this spell works, who will be the moron?"

"You," he said.

Tara turned back to the book and started to chant the words of the spell in a low whisper.

I struggled to hold the heavy book steady. I had one eye on Tara and one eye on the little C-3PO.

Tara squinted hard at the tiny type in the old book. Her lips moved rapidly as she whispered the ancient words.

My arms ached so badly, I thought I might drop the book.

Finally, she finished. She took the book from my hands.

All three of us stared at the action figure. I held my breath. And waited.

And after a few seconds, a strange, frightening rumbling sound rose up from the dresser.

"Oh, wow. I don't *believe* it!" I cried.

16

THE RUMBLING SOUND grew louder.

I jumped back, my heart pounding. I saw the frightened looks on Nicky's and Tara's faces.

Another low rumble.

"Max?" Mom's voice rang out from downstairs. "What's that weird noise up there?"

"Uh . . . it's my stomach," I shouted. "Too much pepperoni on my pizza at lunch!"

Another rumble. The floor trembled.

"Well, go to the bathroom!" Mom shouted.

That's Mom's solution for any problem, whether it makes sense or not. If I say, "Mom, I have a headache," she says go to the bathroom. If I say, "Mom, I broke my arm," she says go to the bathroom.

"Okay," I called down.

Another low rumble. And then the dresser started to move.

I saw it shake. It tilted a bit. The C-3PO figure fell onto its side.

"Oh nooo!" I cried out when I saw the wooden legs of the dresser start to move.

The front legs lifted off the floor. The back legs pushed the dresser forward.

"It—it's moving!" I screamed.

Then the four legs shuffled together, moving like dog legs. The dresser was coming after us!

Tara jumped back, dropped the book, and clapped her hands to her cheeks. "But—but—the action figure!" she cried.

"Forget the action figure," Nicky said. "You brought the *dresser* to life!"

17

THUD. THUD. THUD.

The dresser took slow, steady, *heavy* steps forward.

"Stop it! Stop it! Do something!" I shouted.

"Wh-wh-wh—" For once, Tara was speechless.

"The spell!" Nicky cried. "Read the spell again! Try it! Go ahead!"

Thud. Thud. Thud.

The dresser was in the center of the room now. Moving toward the doorway.

"I—I can't believe it worked!" Tara finally found her voice. She grinned. "Hey, am I powerful or what?"

"*Just stop it!*" I cried.

Thud. Thud. Thud.

She picked up the book and opened it. She raised it close to her face. Her lips started moving as she whispered the ancient words once again.

Thud. Thud. Thud.

The drawers bounced as the dresser made its way to the bedroom door.

Tara finished reading the spell and slammed the book shut. And with the *clap* of the book closing, the dresser stopped.

We stared at it in silence, not breathing.

It didn't move.

It was no longer alive.

Nicky's whole body shook. "Th-that was terrifying!" he said.

"It was horrible!" I cried.

"That was *outstanding*!" Tara exclaimed. "I can't wait to try it again!"

"Max—what's all the racket?" Mom shouted from downstairs. "It sounds like the house is coming down!"

"I . . . uh . . . fell!" I said. "I think I hurt my leg."

"Go to the bathroom!" she shouted.

18

THE NEXT AFTERNOON was cloudy and cool. A strong breeze blew against Quentin and me as we jogged out to the playground for recess.

"When can I come over to show you some magic tricks?" Quentin asked.

"Maybe tomorrow. I'll ask my mom again," I said.

Most of the kids in our class joined in a dodgeball game on the basketball court behind the school. Quentin and I leaned against the wall and watched.

Kids screamed and laughed. They tried to twist and squirm out of the way of the ball. The Wilbur brothers—Willy and Billy—are the champs at dodgeball. That's because they're the meanest kids in school.

They heave the ball into kids' guts so hard, the poor kids walk bent over for the rest of the day! Usually, a good shot in the stomach from the Wilbur brothers means you don't breathe for at least an hour.

When they knock someone out, Willy and Billy go crazy, laughing and slapping each other high fives. They think dodgeball is all about breaking ribs and collapsing lungs.

Do you get the idea that this is *not* my favorite sport?

That's why Quentin and I were watching from the sidelines. We listened to the screams and cries of pain. And we watched kids get hit and go down and lie on the ground groaning and moaning.

Quentin pulled out his deck of cards. "Here's a new trick you'll like, Max," he said. But before he could start, Coach Freeley appeared.

Coach Freeley is our coach and gym teacher. He's built like a tank. He's very short and very wide, with bulging muscles everywhere you can have muscles.

The girls all like him because he's young, and he has lots of wavy black hair and a flashy smile.

He wasn't smiling at Quentin and me.

"You two loafers," he barked, "get in the game!"

"Uh . . . I'm not allowed to play this sport," I told him. "I can't be hit by a ball. I'm allergic to rubber. My skin breaks out."

"Remind me to cry later," Coach Freeley said. He gave us a shove. "No standing around. Get in the game."

Quentin and I joined the circle of kids. I tried

72

to use Quentin as a shield, but he danced away from me.

My hands were sweaty. My heart raced. I *hate* this game. It's as bad as being pounded by Colin.

Willy Wilbur heaved the ball at the kid next to me. The kid tried to leap out of the way. The ball slammed hard into his knee. I heard a loud *crack,* and the kid went down howling.

Billy and Willy laughed and congratulated each other.

The ball bounced twice on the pavement and into my hands.

"Heave it, Max!" Quentin shouted.

I pulled back my arm—aimed at Willy Wilbur's gut—and tossed the ball with all my might.

"Oh noooo!"

Too hard. The ball flew over Willy's head and out toward the playground.

No. No. No.

Traci Wayne came walking by. Traci, the most beautiful, hottest, coolest, most awesome girl in school.

Am I in love with Traci? I don't know. I only know I got all out of breath and almost swallowed my tongue twice the last time I tried to talk to her.

Traci came walking by—and the ball hit her smack in the face.

She let out a startled "Huh?" Blood poured from her perfect nose. And she dropped to her knees in the grass, shaking her blond hair, totally stunned.

"It was an accident!" I shouted. I took off running toward her.

I had been planning to invite her to my birthday party next month.

But maybe this wasn't the best time.

She was holding her head and howling in pain. Blood flowed from her nose, through her fingers.

"An accident," I choked out. "I wasn't aiming. Really. I don't know my own strength. I'm just too awesomely powerful. That's why I don't play dodgeball. It isn't fair to the others."

I don't think she heard me. She was howling at the top of her lungs. Maybe she had a concussion or something.

I bent down to help her up. But I stopped when I saw a figure at the side of the school building. A figure dressed in black.

The evil boy!

He followed me to school!

Pressed against the brick wall, he stared at me.

I saw Mrs. Wright, the principal, running over to help Traci. "Traci, are you okay?" she called.

"Noooo," Traci replied, still covering her face. "Noooooo."

"Mrs. Wright, can I ask you a question?" I said. "Is there a new kid in school? A kid who wears black?"

She squinted at me. "No, Max. The only new kid in school is Quentin Jones."

I turned to Quentin. He was still in the dodgeball game.

"Well, do you see that kid in black over there?" I asked, pointing.

Mrs. Wright looked toward the school.

No one there. The boy in black was gone.

"My faaaaace," Traci Wayne chimed in. "It's broken. It's broken."

Mrs. Wright pulled Traci to her feet. "I don't see any kid in black, Max," she said. "I have to help Traci now." She hurried away, guiding Traci toward the nurse's office.

I turned back to the school and saw the kid again.

A chill ran down my back.

No one else seemed to notice him. He stood there pressed against the building. Watching me . . .

Watching me . . .

Late that night, sound asleep in my bed, I felt a hand grip my shoulder.

19

"**HUH?**" **I JERKED UP** with a startled cry. "Who's there?" I called out in a choked whisper.

The little lamp on my dresser flashed on. Blinking, I saw Tara beside me, her hand on my shoulder. Nicky stood by my dresser, his body tensed, his face tight with worry.

I forced myself to wake up. "What's going on?" I asked.

"Time to go to war," Tara whispered.

"We're going to chase away those ghouls," Nicky said. "Before they do any more damage."

I climbed to my feet, yawning. My pajama pants were all twisted. I nearly fell over. I untwisted them and turned to the two ghosts. "I'll come with you," I said.

Tara pushed me back. "No way, Max."

"We told you before," Nicky said. "Humans can't chase away ghouls. They aren't afraid of humans."

I swallowed. My mouth felt totally dry. "But they're afraid of ghosts?" I asked.

"We hope so," Tara said. Her voice trembled. "We're new at this ghost thing. We don't really know what we're doing."

"It might be a tough fight," Nicky said, brushing back his dark hair.

"But we're doing it for *you*," Tara said, squeezing my shoulder again. "Because we like you, Max. And we know you're our friend."

"Our friend who won't move away and leave us," Nicky added.

I swallowed again. I could see they both were frightened. "Maybe you don't need to fight them," I said. "Maybe the ghouls will just go away."

"Ghouls *never* just go away," Tara replied. "Once they've found a cozy place to live and make mischief, they stay forever."

"But—but—"

Were these ghouls really vicious? I didn't want my friends to get hurt.

"Don't worry, Max," Tara said. "We'll sneak up on them. We'll scare them to death."

Nicky smacked his fist against his palm. "They won't know what hit them," he said. "Bam, boom. They're history." Tough words—but I noticed his voice cracked.

I started toward the door. "I'm coming with you."

Tara pushed me back again. "Hel-*lo*. How can we surprise them if you come with us?"

"Okay, okay." I dropped back onto my bed.

Nicky clicked off the dresser lamp. We were left in a deep darkness.

Then the two ghosts disappeared into the hall.

"Good luck," I whispered.

They didn't reply.

I stared into the blackness, hugging myself to stop my shivers. I sat up straight, alert to every sound.

I waited . . . and I listened.

20

THE SILENCE RANG in my ears.

I shut my eyes and tried to picture what the two ghouls looked like. How did Nicky and Tara plan to scare them? Did my friends really believe the ghouls would just turn and run?

My heart started to beat like a bass drum. I clasped my hands together. They were wet and cold.

I should have talked them out of this, I decided. What makes them think they can fight two vicious ghouls?

The questions kept repeating in my mind as I listened to the silence. Staring into the blackness, I just wanted it to be over.

Silence.

Silence. So quiet I could hear the hum of the refrigerator as it clicked on downstairs.

More silence.

And then a loud *thud* made me jump to my feet.

I heard a choked gasp. Another *thud*.

I shut my eyes tight. My hands were squeezed into tight fists. My pajama shirt was damp, clinging to my back.

I heard a hard bump. The sound of someone hitting the floor. More gasps. More thuds.

And then a high, shrill laugh. Not a human laugh at all. An eerie laugh like an ambulance siren, rising and falling.

I jumped to my feet and staggered to the doorway. I poked my head out into the hall.

I heard scrapes and bumps, sounds of a struggle. But I couldn't see a thing.

I heard a soft cry. And then a long, scraping sound—like someone sliding down the banister.

Another shrill laugh. More hard bumps. Someone being heaved into the wall? Were they wrestling now?

I jammed my hands over my ears. I couldn't stand it. My legs were trembling. I had to lean against the doorframe to keep from falling.

I pictured my poor friends being beaten by two hideous ghouls. Wrestling on the hall rug. Being smothered by the creatures.

Even with my hands pressed over my ears, I could hear the bumps and thuds of the battle.

And then silence again.

I lowered my hands to my sides. I hunched tensely in my bedroom doorway, every muscle tight.

Silence. That ringing, hollow silence.

I couldn't move. I couldn't breathe.

"Nicky?" I called down the hall in a hoarse whisper. "Nicky? Tara? Are you okay?"

No answer.

21

HOW LONG DID THE SILENCE LAST? I don't know. I only know it was the most terrifying silence of my life. And it seemed to go on for *hours*!

And then finally, I heard the scrape of shoes on the hall rug. A cough. A soft groan.

Footsteps approaching me.

"Nicky? Tara? Is that you?"

Or was it the ghouls?

Listening to the slow footsteps, I staggered back into my room. I clicked on the ceiling light.

Nicky stepped into the doorway. I saw his hair standing on end as if he'd received an electric shock.

And then I saw that he had an arm around Tara.

He dragged her into my room. She was bent nearly in half. His left arm was wrapped around her waist. And his right arm . . . *his right arm was missing*!

Then Tara stood up—and I opened my mouth in a scream of horror.

"Tara!" I wailed to Nicky. "Her head!"

Her head . . . No head on her shoulders. No head . . .

22

I SUDDENLY FELT DIZZY. I had to turn away.

Nicky dragged his headless sister into the room with his one arm.

"Is she . . . is she . . . ?" I couldn't get any words out.

"I'm okay," Tara said.

"Huh?" I gasped and stared at her shoulders—and at the spot above them, where her head should have been.

"My head is just invisible," she said. "The fight with the ghouls used up a lot of energy."

Nicky dropped Tara beside me on the bed. "My arm will come back too," he said. "It's still there. See?" He reached out and touched my head with his invisible hand.

"Why didn't you warn me?" I shouted. "You . . . you scared me to death!"

I heard Tara sigh. "I wish we'd scared the *ghouls* to death. It would have been a lot easier."

I stared at her headless shoulders. "You mean . . . they're still here?"

84

Nicky squeezed his invisible arm. "No. They're gone. But frightening them didn't work. We had to fight them."

"How?" I asked.

Tara's face glimmered faintly. I could see her ears and her dangling earrings, and a little of her dark hair. Slowly, her head was coming back into view.

She brushed a strand of hair off her forehead. "They tried to smother us. They had big, blobby bodies. Sticky like bubble gum. They stuck themselves to our faces. We couldn't breathe."

"How'd you get them off?" I asked.

"We blew bubbles," Nicky said.

Tara chuckled. "It was kinda funny. We blew big bubble gum bubbles in their skin—and popped them."

"That made big holes in the ghouls' bodies," Nicky said, still squeezing his missing arm. "They didn't like that. They made these horrible squealing sounds. Then they unstuck themselves from us and ran out the front door."

"I don't think we'll see them again," Tara said.

I let out a long whoosh of breath. "Thanks, guys," I said. "You really were awesome. You . . . you risked everything for me. I know you're dead, but you risked your *lives* for me!"

Tara's face came back completely. "Well, we don't want to lose you," she said. She grinned at me.

I suddenly felt guilty. How could I *think* of leaving them here all alone?

"I don't want to lose you, either," I said. "You're my best friends. You fought for me. You saved me from those ghouls. I don't want to move to Texas and leave you here. I want to stay and help you, the way you helped me."

"Thanks, Max," Nicky said. "We were hoping you'd say that."

"You're all we've got," Tara said.

"Maybe we can find a way to stop my dad from moving us," I said.

Nicky and Tara vanished a few minutes after that. I tried to get back to sleep, but no way. I kept picturing them struggling with sticky, blobby ghouls. My stomach did a flip-flop each time I remembered Tara being helped into my room without a head.

I was still wide awake when Mom shouted upstairs that it was time to get dressed for school. Yawning, I pulled on jeans and a T-shirt and dragged myself into the kitchen.

Mom set down the phone and greeted me with a big smile. "Good news, Maxie," she said. "The Marvins have decided to buy our house!"

23

THE SCHOOL DAY WENT BY in an unhappy blur. I couldn't think about anything except the Marvins moving into our house. And me leaving Nicky and Tara and moving to Texas.

Leaving them after they'd risked their lives for me . . .

I saw that Traci Wayne wasn't in class, so I asked Ms. McDonald about her. She said that Traci had finally stopped howling. But her face was red and swollen. Her mom had said she looked like an overripe tomato. So she wasn't ready to come back to school.

I still wanted to invite her to my birthday party next month. But what if my birthday party was in Texas?

After school, I found Nicky and Tara waiting for me in my room. They both looked pale and worried.

"We have to do something," Nicky said. "We

have to find a way to stop your parents from moving."

Tara tugged her hat down over her ears. "Max, what if you told your mom about us? She might feel sorry for Nicky and me, and—"

I shook my head. "My mom doesn't believe in ghosts," I said. "I tried to tell her about you weeks ago. She told me to stop making up stories. If I tell her again, she'll just say I'm making up a dumb story because I don't want to move."

"But what if Nicky and I *proved* to her that we exist?" Tara said.

Nicky stopped pacing. His dark eyes flashed with excitement. "Yeah, dude. Your mom can't see us. But there are *lots* of ways we can *show* her we're in the room."

I rested my head in my hands and thought hard. Maybe . . . maybe it would work.

Maybe we could prove to Mom that two ghost kids were in the house. And that they really needed our help. That we were the only ones who could help them . . .

Then maybe Mom would talk Dad into staying here.

I jumped to my feet. "Okay. Let's try it," I said.

They followed me downstairs. We found Mom in the den. She sat on the brown leather couch with her feet up on the coffee table. She had opera on the CD player, and she was reading a book.

She raised her head and smiled as I walked in. She patted the cushion next to her.

"You know, this room is so comfy and cozy. I really love this house," she said. "I'm kind of sorry to leave it too."

"Uh . . . that's what I wanted to talk to you about," I said. I sat down next to her.

Mom hummed along with the opera.

My heart started to pound. My mouth suddenly felt dry.

"Go ahead, Max," Tara said. "Tell her."

"Tell her we're standing right here," Nicky said.

"I'm getting to it," I said. "Give me a chance."

Mom frowned at me. "Getting to *what,* Max?"

"Well . . ." I took a deep breath. "I have something important to tell you. . . ."

24

MOM BRUSHED THE HAIR off my forehead.

I have very bouncy hair. It plopped back over my eyebrows.

Mom brushed it back again, and it bounced over my face again.

She gave up and smiled. "What is it, Max? You look so worried."

"We can't move," I blurted out.

Her smile faded. "Max, please—"

"We can't leave because of my two ghost friends," I said. I started talking as fast as I could. I wanted to get it all out before Mom told me I was crazy again.

"There are two ghosts who live in this house, Mom, and they're my friends. I'm the only one who can see and hear them. And they need me. They need me to stay here with them. I have to stay here until their parents return."

Mom shook her head slowly. She grabbed my hand and squeezed it. "Maxie, I'm sorry you're afraid of moving away from here," she said softly. "But it will be okay. I promise."

"Mom, you don't understand," I said. "It's not because I'm afraid. I'm not making this up. Really."

"Maxie, listen to me. Your ghost stories—"

"I'm going to prove it," I said, jumping to my feet. "If I prove there are ghosts here, will you listen to me, Mom?"

Mom closed her book. She stared up at me.

"You're going to prove there are ghosts in the room? Is this one of your magic tricks?"

"No way," I said. "No tricks. It's for real."

She crossed her arms in front of her. "Go ahead. I'm game. Prove it to me."

I took a deep breath.

She really was listening this time.

I turned to Nicky and Tara. I couldn't see them. Sometimes they go invisible.

"Tara," I said, "pick up my mom's book. Make it float around the room."

The book sat on Mom's lap. She moved her hands away from it. We both stared down at the book.

"Nothing's happening," Mom said.

"Go ahead, Tara," I said. "Show my mom you're here. Make the book float up in the air."

Mom and I both waited.

I counted to ten.

"Nicky? Tara? Where are you?" I asked, gazing around. I didn't see them anywhere.

"Max, are you *sure* this isn't some kind of magic trick?" Mom asked. "It isn't working too well."

"It's not a trick," I snapped. "Nicky? Tara? Stop kidding around. Pick up the couch pillows. Make them fly back and forth around the room. Come on. Hurry!"

Mom turned and stared at the pillows. "Max? I don't get it," she said. "Is this a joke?"

"Nicky? Tara?" I cried, my voice cracking. "Show Mom you're here. Come on. Make the pillows fly."

Nothing.

"Nicky? Tara?"

I picked up a pillow. I tossed it into the air. "Nicky—catch!"

The pillow dropped to the floor. I picked it up and tossed it high again. "The ghosts are throwing it!" I said. "Look, Mom." I tossed the pillow again.

"Max, give it up," Mom said.

"But—but—but—" I sputtered. "I don't understand it. They were here a minute ago. I—"

She got to her feet. She wrapped me in a hug and pressed her cheek against mine. It felt warm and soft.

"Maxie, listen to me," she whispered. "I know moving away is a scary thing. Especially moving far away. But you don't have to make up ghost stories to change our minds."

"But Mom—"

"We'll all be together," Mom said. "Think of the move as a big adventure for *all* of us."

"Okay, Mom," I whispered.

What else could I say? Nicky and Tara had suddenly vanished. It happened to them all the time. They said they couldn't help it. But this was the *worst* possible time.

And so Mom thought I was a big baby, making up ghost stories so she'd feel sorry for me.

I had no choice. I turned and trudged up to my room.

"Nicky? Tara?" I called, closing my bedroom door behind me. "Are you in here? Where did you go? Are you okay? Why did you disappear?"

No reply.

I sank onto my bed. *Now* what? I asked myself.

I can't move to Texas and leave my good friends all alone in the world.

But what can I do about it?

25

AFTER SCHOOL THE NEXT DAY, Quentin finally came home with me. I was really excited that he and I could finally share some tricks.

I left him in the kitchen and hurried up to my bedroom. "Nicky? Tara? Are you back?" I cried. I glanced around the room.

I still hadn't seen them since they'd disappeared in the den. I was starting to worry about them.

I sighed. No sign of them.

I hurried down to the kitchen and pulled out some snacks. "Watch this trick," I said to Quentin. "Bet I can make this cookie disappear."

We made a whole bunch of cookies disappear. Then we went up to my room to show each other magic tricks.

Quentin had brought over a black leather bag filled with his magic stuff. He set it down next to my desk. "You go first," he said. "Let's see what you've got."

I did a few simple sight tricks first. I made a quarter disappear, and I pulled it from his ear. I took scissors and cut a piece of rope into three sections. Then I made the rope appear whole again. I waved a magic wand, and the wand turned into a bouquet of flowers.

Baby stuff.

Quentin watched me the whole time with his arms crossed in front of him. His shiny blue eyes studied my tricks without blinking. He was concentrating hard.

I finished with one of my harder tricks. I borrowed Quentin's baseball cap. I poured a pitcher of water into it. Then I swung the cap over him and pulled it down onto his head.

No water. The cap was totally dry.

"Not bad," he said. "Very cool."

I grinned. "Thanks. I had a lot of accidents with that trick. But now I get it right *most* of the time."

Quentin brushed back his blond hair. "Show me how to do it?" he asked.

"First show me your stuff," I said. I dropped down on the edge of my bed to watch.

He bent down to open his black case. He turned his back to block my view. He placed a lot of stuff on the desk. When he turned around, he had an egg in his hand.

"I do a lot of card tricks," he said. "But you

probably know them all. So I'm going to start off with my best trick."

He held up the egg. "Keep your eye on the egg, Max. Don't let it out of your sight."

I leaned forward, resting my head in my hands, and gazed up at the egg.

He stuck his hand out and shoved the egg toward my face. Then he pulled it back and swung his arm around twice. He closed his fist around the egg, hiding it.

"Are you watching?" he asked. "This is a trick I've been hatching for a long time."

I stared at Quentin's fist. "Ta-daa!" he sang.

He opened his hand—and in his palm sat a live chick.

"Wow!" I cried. I jumped up from the bed and took a closer look. It really was a live chick. "Awesome!" I said. "That's outstanding!"

Quentin grinned. He took a short bow. Then he turned and carefully set the chick down inside the bag.

"Did you have it in your sleeve?" I asked. "Or did you have it in your other hand the whole time?"

Before he could answer, the bedroom door swung open and Colin came bouncing in. He grinned his perfect, toothy grin at me as he checked out Quentin's magic gear on my desk.

"Yo! Magic tricks," he said. He turned to Quentin. "I'm into magic too."

"No way," Quentin said.

Colin strode up to me. "Want to see a really neat trick? I can make parts of Max's skin turn bright red."

"No, please—" I cried. I tried to scramble away. Too late.

Pow powpow powpowpow.

Colin jerked up my T-shirt. He grinned at Quentin. "See?"

My stomach and chest were bright red.

"G-good trick," I sputtered, when I could finally breathe again.

"Here's a better one," Quentin told my brother.

He stepped up close to Colin and cupped a hand over his own right eye. He twisted his hand a few times.

Then Quentin pulled his hand away and raised his palm in front of Colin's face.

Resting in Quentin's palm was his *eyeball*!

"Gaaaack!" Colin opened his mouth and let out a choking sound. His eyes bulged as he stared in horror at Quentin's runny, wet eyeball. The blue eye seemed to stare up at him.

"No way!" Colin gasped. He turned and took off, running out of the room. A few seconds later, we heard loud groans and heaves—violent vomiting sounds—coming from his room.

Quentin giggled as he pushed the eyeball back into place.

I gaped at him. "How did you do that?"

A sly smile crossed his face. "Wouldn't *you* like to know!"

26

QUENTIN REFUSED TO SHOW ME how to do any of his tricks. He said he had to hurry home for dinner. "Next time, we'll trade secrets," he said.

He packed up his bag and I showed him downstairs. We could still hear Colin gagging and retching in his room.

I figured any trick that could make my brother lose his lunch was a totally excellent trick. I wanted to learn it as soon as possible. It looked so totally real. But I knew it couldn't be.

"How about tomorrow?" I asked Quentin.

He shrugged. "Maybe." He took off jogging to the street, swinging the black leather bag beside him.

I went into the kitchen, borrowed an egg from the fridge, and carried it upstairs to my room. I practiced sliding it around in my hand. I tried to figure out how Quentin had palmed it and made a chick appear in its place.

Then I realized that the chick couldn't have

been hidden in his sleeve. He'd been wearing a short-sleeved T-shirt!

I set the egg down. I couldn't figure it out. Maybe Quentin will show me how it's done tomorrow, I thought.

I heard a car rumble outside. I heard a horn. Two long blasts.

I poked my head out the window and saw Mom's car turning into the drive. I ran outside to greet her.

"Help me with these grocery bags," she said, popping the trunk. "Oh, I'm in a state. I'm late. I can't believe this is happening."

"Huh? What's happening?" I asked.

She dropped a bulging grocery bag into my hands. It weighed about fifty pounds and sent me staggering to my knees.

Buster began barking his head off in the garage. I guess he just wanted to be let out to say hi to Mom.

"No time. No time," Mom said, fluttering around like a hummingbird. "Hurry. Take that bag in and come out for more."

I started to the kitchen door. "But what's going on, Mom?" I asked from behind the bag.

"It's Mr. Grimmus," she replied, following me inside. "Your dad's new boss from Dallas. He's surprised us. He's coming for dinner *tonight*."

"Oh, wow," I muttered. I dropped the grocery

bag onto the kitchen counter. "He's coming to check Dad out for the job?"

"That's right," Mom said. "He likes to surprise people. Drop in on them without any warning."

She began walking around in fast circles, rubbing her chin almost raw, talking to herself. "What should I do first? Should we have chicken or steak? Chicken or steak?"

Buster barked and howled in the garage.

"Steak!" Mom snapped her fingers. "I'll throw the steaks on. I bought fresh steaks the other day. We have a freezer full of them." She flashed me a tense smile. "Mr. Grimmus is from Texas, right? He'll like a good steak."

"I guess," I said weakly. I wasn't thinking about steaks. I was thinking about Nicky and Tara.

"Yes. Steaks. Good old steaks!" Mom said. "So easy. So quick. And perfect for a Texan."

She pulled open the freezer door—and let out a groan.

I sniffed the air. "Oh, gross!" I moaned. "What's that pukey smell? It smells like a *skunk*!"

Mom gripped the freezer door and peered inside. Her chin was trembling. Her eyes watered. "Broken," she whispered. "The freezer is broken."

She let go of the door and began pounding her fists against the side of the fridge. "Spoiled! All the steaks—they're spoiled!" she screamed. She pounded the fridge like a crazy person.

"Mom—stop!" I cried, holding my nose against the heavy putrid odor. I grabbed her around the waist and pulled her away from the fridge.

"The steaks are rotten," she moaned. "Rotten! They turned green. Do you believe it? They're *green*!" She tried to beat the fridge again, but I held her away.

She rubbed her chin again, thinking hard. "What am I going to serve Mr. Grimmus?" she asked. "If we don't make a good impression, your dad will lose the job!"

In the garage, Buster howled and barked. Maybe he smelled the rotten meat.

Mom grabbed the car keys and ran to the kitchen door. "When your dad gets home, tell him I'm at the butcher shop!"

The door slammed behind her.

Nicky and Tara were waiting in my bedroom. Nicky was pacing back and forth with his hands clasped behind his back. Tara was stretched out on my bed with the old spell book open on her lap.

"You're back!" I cried. "Where were you? Why did you leave me there in the den?"

"Sorry, Max," Tara said, looking up from the book. "We keep fading away. We can't control it." She sighed. "Everything just goes black."

"Well, what are we going to do?" I asked. "Did you hear my mom? Did you hear what's happening?"

"We heard everything," Nicky said, shaking his head.

"That's why I'm looking up spells," Tara said, turning the page in her book. "There *has* to be a spell for keeping Texans out of the house."

"Ha, ha," I said, frowning at her. "Remind me to laugh later." I sighed and dropped down on the edge of the bed. "I repeat my question. What are we going to do?"

Tara's eyes flashed. "Maybe we should bring back those two ghouls."

"No way!" I said. "My parents would *kill* me. You know I'd get blamed. I'd be a ghost like you. Really."

"Just kidding," Tara said. "The ghouls are gone."

My throat felt tight. It was hard to swallow, hard to breathe. "I . . . don't want to leave you guys," I said. "But if Mr. Grimmus likes us, I . . . I'm gone."

Before they could reply, the front doorbell rang.

"That's him!" I cried. "That's Mr. Grimmus."

Colin poked his head into my room. "Let's go, loser face," he said. "That's Dad's new boss. We've gotta go make nice. I know *you* won't make a good impression. But at least he'll see that *I'm* a winner."

I checked my hair in the mirror. A bouncy mess, as always. I took a deep breath. "Okay, I'm coming," I said.

I turned and saw Colin staring at my bed. His eyes bulged. "Max," he said, pointing. "That big book . . . it's floating in midair."

"Yes, I know," I said. "It's such a good book. I can't put it down!"

27

I FOLLOWED COLIN DOWN the stairs. Dad was shaking hands with Mr. Grimmus at the front door.

He was a big red-faced man with long wavy white hair and a bushy white mustache. He wore a tight-fitting brown suit and a vest that barely covered his big belly. He had a black string tie around the collar of his white shirt, and he wore high-heeled black cowboy boots.

Dad was wearing his best suit, which was also his only suit. Mom is always after him to buy more dress-up clothes. But Dad always argues, "I don't need dress-up clothes to go to the wrestling matches."

That's about the only time Dad takes Mom out. When the wrestling matches come to the arena downtown.

"I always fly first class," Mr. Grimmus was telling my dad. He patted his big belly. "I don't like to be fenced in."

Dad laughed really loud, as if Mr. Grimmus had just told a terrific joke.

Then Dad saw Colin and me on the stairway. "Mr. Grimmus, here are my two sons, Colin and Max," he said.

Mr. Grimmus shook hands with Colin. He squeezed Colin's hand so hard, I heard my brother's ears pop.

Then the big Texan turned to me. "How ya doin', ol' hoss?" He slapped me hard on the back. I only choked for two or three minutes.

Dad led the way into the living room. Mr. Grimmus' boots thundered on the floor as we walked. When he sat down, he took up almost the whole couch. He unbuttoned his vest and his stomach popped out like a balloon.

"Where's the little lady?" he asked, glancing around.

"She went out for a moment," Dad said. "She wants dinner tonight to be special."

"I can't wait," Mr. Grimmus said, rubbing his hands together. "I'm so hungry, I could eat a calf."

Dad laughed really hard again. I could see that he was totally tense. Usually, he only laughs at Colin making fun of me.

Mr. Grimmus turned to Colin and me. "What sports do you play?" he asked Colin.

Colin leaned forward in his chair and cracked his knuckles. "Well, I'm all-state in three sports," he said. "Football, basketball, and track."

"If chasing girls is a sport," Dad said, "Colin is all-state in that, too!"

He and Mr. Grimmus tossed back their heads and laughed really hard at that. Mr. Grimmus' face turned even redder than before.

He turned to me. "And what do *you* do?"

"I clap for Colin," I said.

I meant it as a joke. But this time, no one laughed.

Colin sneaked his big shoe over mine and stepped down hard on my foot.

"Ow!" I let out a cry. I couldn't help it.

That made Colin dig his heel into the top of my sneaker. Pain shot up my leg. But I gritted my teeth and didn't say anything.

Mr. Grimmus squinted at me. His mustache twitched. "You wouldn't kid an old cowboy, would you, Max? What sports *do* you play?"

"Well . . . I made captain of the math team this year," I said.

Mr. Grimmus smiled at Colin. "I guess there's only one athlete in this family," he said. "How fast do you run the four-forty, boy?"

"I hold the school record," Colin said, cracking his knuckles again.

I saw Dad glaring at me. I knew I was letting him down. He wanted me to impress his new boss too. He didn't want Mr. Grimmus to know that I'm a helpless wimp.

I took a deep breath and decided to give it another try. "Uh . . . the kids at school all call me Brainimon," I said. "That's because I'm at the top of my class."

Mr. Grimmus' bulby red nose twitched. "Brainimon? What kinda word is that? Is that some kinda foreign language?" He grinned. "The only foreign language I speak is Texan! *Haw, haw, haw.*"

He and Dad practically busted a gut over that one.

After that, everyone grew silent. It was totally tense. I could see that Dad wanted to keep the conversation going, but he couldn't think of anything else to say.

Mr. Grimmus tapped a rhythm on his knees with his big hands. He started to whistle to himself.

Colin cracked his knuckles again.

"Uh . . . ," Dad started. I could see his eyes spinning. He knew this wasn't going well. "Nice day," he said finally.

Mr. Grimmus nodded. "Hot as a prairie dog's behind," he said.

That didn't make any sense to me. But I kept quiet.

"Supposed to be a nice spring," Dad added. Sweat was rolling down his forehead. He mopped his bald head with one hand.

Looking over Mr. Grimmus' shoulder, I saw

Nicky and Tara come down the stairs. Tara had the big spell book under one arm.

Panic swept over me. They're going to get me in horrible trouble, I thought. Of course, I don't want to move away. But if something goes wrong with this dinner tonight, I'll be blamed.

And then *I'll* be the dead meat around here. Mom and Dad will *kill* me!

My brain spun wildly. I felt totally helpless. Yes, I wanted to stay here. No, I didn't want the ghosts to get me in major trouble tonight.

"Go away!" I shouted, waving them back.

Mr. Grimmus' mouth dropped open. "Sorry, ol' hoss. I didn't hear you correctly."

Nicky and Tara stopped at the bottom of the stairs.

"I mean it. Go away," I said.

Mr. Grimmus scowled at me. He jumped to his feet. "I don't understand, young man. I—"

Dad's eyes burned angrily into mine. "Max, what is your problem?"

"I . . . I was talking to that fly," I said. I pretended to swat at a fly. "It's been buzzing around my head." I swatted again. "Go away, fly. I mean it. Go away!"

Colin chuckled. "Max is an artist," he told Mr. Grimmus. "He draws flies."

Dad laughed at that one. But Mr. Grimmus just stared at me.

Colin tromped down hard on my foot again.

Mr. Grimmus was still standing in front of the couch, his huge belly hovering over the coffee table. Suddenly, he turned to the stairs and his eyes nearly bulged out of his head.

He let out a gasp and pointed. "That book—it's floating down the stairs by itself!"

I darted across the room and grabbed the book out of Tara's hands.

Dad, Colin, and Mr. Grimmus were all staring at me.

"It's a book about helium balloons," I said. "Very clever how they do that, isn't it?"

They kept staring.

Luckily, Mom stuck her head out the kitchen door. "Dinner is served, gentlemen," she announced. "Please, everyone come in."

Whew. A close call.

I followed everyone into the dining room. I had my fingers crossed. Would dinner with Mr. Grimmus go okay, without any disasters?

Three guesses.

28

MR. GRIMMUS REACHED OVER the table and slapped Dad on the back. "You've got a fine little filly here, Doyle!" he boomed. He grinned at Mom.

Mom lowered her head and gave him a shy smile.

"I'm loving these chops," Mr. Grimmus said. "I could eat me a whole side of lamb. *Haw, haw.*"

Dad laughed with him. Mom started to choke on her salad. But she covered up pretty well.

"I'm glad you're enjoying your dinner, Mr. Grimmus," Mom said. "Your visit was a big surprise. But I tried to whip up something you'd like."

Mr. Grimmus swallowed a mountain of mashed potatoes. "I like your family, Doyle," he said, nodding at Dad. "You pass the family test. I think y'all will do really fine in Texas."

"I'm pretty proud of them too," Dad said. He smiled at Mom and Colin.

The dinner was going well. But I felt so totally weird. Dad never talked like that in his life. He sounded so stiff and tense. And he looked so strange, wearing a necktie at the dinner table. Sometimes, when we had no company, he didn't even wear a shirt!

"I did a social studies unit on Texas last year," Colin said. "I wrote a paper about cattle ranchers and how they fought against sheepherders. It was totally interesting."

You go, Colin! My bro was really working the charm. And Mr. Grimmus was eating it up.

"Luckily, my family was in the barbed wire business," Mr. Grimmus said. "Those ranchers all needed fences. They made us as rich as the filling in a pecan pie!"

He and Dad shared another big laugh.

"Well, I loved reading about Texas," Colin continued. "I can't wait to see it in person."

Whoa. My brother was really going for the gold star tonight!

"I'll take you out to my ranch," Mr. Grimmus told Colin. "I've got a hundred and thirty-three different kinds of cactus there. I think you'll find that very interesting."

"You got that right," Colin replied.

"Is it cactus or cacti?" I chimed in.

Mr. Grimmus frowned at me. "You'll know if you *sit* on one, boy!" he exclaimed.

Everyone laughed at that one. I tried to fake some laughter too. Just to show I was a good sport.

I kept glancing at Mom and then at Dad. They didn't really *like* this big, loudmouthed balloon— *did* they?

At least the dinner was going smoothly. No ghouls. No spilled sour milk or pies in the face.

Maybe I'd get out of it alive.

Mr. Grimmus seemed to be enjoying himself a lot. And I could see that Dad was happy. He was passing the test.

Mom offered Mr. Grimmus the platter of lamb chops. Then she served more mashed potatoes and string beans.

Mr. Grimmus was telling us about his family. He had seven children by his first wife, and seven children by his second wife.

"I guess seven is my lucky number!" he exclaimed.

"Or maybe fourteen," I said.

He squinted at me. "No, hoss. Seven. Seven has always been my lucky number. Not fourteen. I know you're a math freak, but don't try to change my lucky number."

"Sorry," I muttered.

Mr. Grimmus picked up a lamb chop and raised it high. "This is lamb chop number seven," he said. "See? My lucky night." He chomped into the chop.

I finished my glass of apple juice. I glanced toward the kitchen.

And to my surprise, I saw the freezer door at the top of the fridge swing open.

At first, I thought I was imagining things. But no. The freezer had opened up.

A few seconds later, I saw Mr. Grimmus set down his lamb chop and sniff the air.

He made a face. He sniffed the air again. He made another face.

"You smell something?" he asked.

29

MOM AND DAD SNIFFED. They both made disgusted faces.

Colin sniffed. He pinched his fingers over his nose and laughed. "Max isn't toilet trained," he said.

"Shut up!" I cried.

Colin waved a big fist at me. "Who's gonna make me?"

"Boys—please!" Mom shouted. "We don't want to give Mr. Grimmus the wrong idea about you two."

Dad glared angrily at me. "I'm warning you. No trouble," he said through gritted teeth.

Mr. Grimmus wasn't paying any attention to us. He had covered his nose with a checkered handkerchief. "Something rotten here," he muttered. His eyes began to water.

In the kitchen, I saw a package of spoiled, green meat fall out of the open freezer. It landed with a soft *plop,* and the shrink-wrap package broke open.

"Uh, Mom . . . ," I started, pointing to the freezer.

"Shhh. Enough out of you, Max," Mom said. "Please be quiet and let us all enjoy our dinner."

Enjoy our dinner? How *could* we, with that disgusting, rank odor floating over the table?

"Mom, please—"

Why wouldn't she let me explain what was happening?

I turned back to the kitchen.

Another package of spoiled meat rolled out of the freezer. And then another.

Plop. Plop.

They landed on top of each other.

The sour, stinging odor floated into the dining room, stronger now. My eyes began to water too.

I held my hand over my mouth. I didn't want to puke.

"How about those Yankees?" Dad said to Mr. Grimmus. "Do you believe they bought another All-Star pitcher?"

Dad was trying to keep things going. But it wasn't going to work. The putrid smell was making us all choke.

"Mom—" I tried again.

But she hushed me with both hands.

In the kitchen, I saw the gross, smelly meat burst from its packaging and make a big, disgusting pile on the kitchen floor.

"Mom—?"

I stared in shock as the pile of meat began to move. At first, I thought it was just toppling over. But then I saw the rancid green hunks squeezing together.

They were forming one big glob of rotten meat.

And then the pile heaved forward.

I heard a sick *squish* as the meat raised itself, moving slowly, silently. The meat piled high, rising to form a shape.

It looked like a snowman! A snowman made out of decayed, stinking meat.

"Uh—uh—uh—" I tried to warn everyone. But I was in shock. No words would come out.

The pile of meat shifted again. Shifted to form a new shape—a human shape with chunky legs and wobbly, trembling meat arms. It rose up as tall as me! And, with a sickening *squish squish*, it came lumbering toward the dining room.

I turned, and behind Mr. Grimmus I saw Nicky and Tara enter the room. Tara had her big spell book under her arm.

"I can't believe you did this!" I screamed. "I can't believe you brought the meat to life!"

Mr. Grimmus leaped up from his chair. "Young man, are you talking to *me*?"

The meat monster staggered into the dining room.

"*Stop* it!" I screamed at Tara. "Make it stop!"

"I . . . I don't know how," she said.

30

MR. GRIMMUS WAS ON HIS FEET. His face turned even redder than before, and his mustache twitched. "Young man, what do you want me to stop?"

"I wasn't talking to you," I said. "I was talking to the meat!"

"Max, please—" Mom said.

But then Mr. Grimmus finally saw the huge meat monster plopping into the dining room. "Whoa!" He staggered back against the dining room wall.

Dad saw it too. "Max, is this one of your tricks? I *warned* you!"

"I didn't do it!" I screamed. "It was Tara. One of the ghosts."

Mr. Grimmus squinted at me. "Ghosts? Is that a ghost walking into the dining room?"

I turned to Nicky and Tara. "Do something!"

The rotten meat creature plopped up to the dining room table.

I couldn't breathe. The sour stink was choking me.

Colin jumped up from his seat, a sick expression on his face. He turned from the table, leaned over his chair, and began to retch noisily, barfing up his lamb chops onto the carpet.

Mr. Grimmus stood pressed against the wall, frozen in wide-eyed horror. Mom and Dad hadn't moved. They stared at the meat monster as it squished and plopped toward them. They were so stunned, their faces were totally blank.

And then I saw Tara hand the spell book to Nicky. She stepped forward, her eyes on the meat creature.

"Go back," she ordered it. "Go back. I created you. And now I'm ordering you to go back!"

"*Aaaagggggh.*" Colin retched up more of his dinner.

Mr. Grimmus' face looked green too. He covered his mouth with his handkerchief.

The meat monster waved its arms and staggered forward.

"Go back! *Back!*" Tara shouted.

"It—it isn't stopping!" I cried.

I tried to jump out of the way, but I was too slow. The disgusting rotten meat creature leaped at me and wrapped its foul body around me.

"Ohhhh." The putrid odor swept over me. I

staggered back, fighting hard, struggling to punch it, to shove it off me, to heave it away.

But the horrible meat clung to me. The cold, chunky arms pressed around my waist. The creature smothered my face. Covered me in spoiled meat.

Still twisting and squirming, I sank to my knees. "Can't . . . breathe . . . ," I choked out.

I knew I didn't have much time. Holding my breath against the overpowering stink, I dove forward and knocked the meat monster to the floor.

As it tightened its clammy hold around my waist, I dug my hands into it—and began frantically pulling out chunk after chunk of the disgusting green meat.

Gasping for breath, I tore at its head. Ripped off one arm and flung it into the kitchen. Dug my hands in and grabbed away a big glob.

Too late.

Too late.

I had no breath left.

It rolled over. Rolled on top of me and covered my face.

I lay on the floor. Gasping . . . gasping . . . My chest about to explode, I was too weak to move. Too weak to fight.

31

SPREADING ITSELF OVER ME, pressing down on my face, the meat creature gurgled and slurped.

"Max—get up!" I heard Dad shouting. He sounded so far away.

And then I heard another sound. A light thud of footsteps.

I heard a growl. More footsteps.

I turned and peered out from under the meat creature—and saw a big, furry animal bound heavily into the room.

Buster!

How did Buster get into the house?

Buster barged into the kitchen. He raised his snout and sniffed the air hard. He lowered his head and saw the meat monster.

Buster's mouth dropped open, and he bared his teeth.

My heart pounding, I froze.

And watched Buster attack.

He leaped onto the meat creature and attacked it—*devoured* it.

122

Buster snarled and dug his teeth in, chewed, and swallowed big hunks of the spoiled meat, swallowed them *whole*.

He downed the whole rotten thing in seconds, just the way he had gobbled up my steak!

Then he sat on his haunches, breathing hard, licking his chops, his big tail scraping the floor. He had bits of spoiled meat stuck to his snout. He licked furiously, enjoying every morsel.

Still flat on my back, I slowly raised my head. "Hunh? Hunnh?" I tried to clear my throat. I had chunks of rotten meat in my hair and smeared on my cheeks and chin.

Blinking hard, I saw Nicky and Tara. Tara gripped the spell book in her hands. "Sorry about that!" she called.

"How could you *do* this to me?" I cried.

Dad reached down and pulled me to my feet. "Who are you talking to?" he asked.

"Uh . . . Buster," I said. "I just wondered how he felt after eating twenty pounds of rotten meat."

Actually, Buster felt just fine. He was still licking his snout, wagging his tail happily. He kept looking up at the freezer. Waiting for more meat to fall out, I guess.

I stood up and followed Dad back to the dining room. Mr. Grimmus pressed his handkerchief over his nose. With his free hand, he was buttoning his vest.

"Thanks for a most . . . unusual dinner," he said to Mom. He started brushing himself off frantically with the handkerchief. He mopped his forehead. Then he wiped his jacket, his vest.

He hurried to the front door. "Oh, the smell," he muttered to himself. "It's like I stepped in cattle plop with both feet. I'll never get it off me!"

"Mr. Grimmus—are you leaving?" Dad cried in alarm. He hurried after him.

"Of *course* I'm leaving!" Mr. Grimmus cried. "Meat coming to life? Do you really think I'm going to hire someone whose house smells like dead cattle and has meat coming to life in the kitchen?"

"But—but—but—the job?" Dad sputtered.

Mr. Grimmus turned at the front door. "Let me put it in the nicest way possible," he said. "Don't ever cross my path again. And don't ever come to Texas!"

He slammed the door behind him.

Dad slumped back into the dining room. Colin was still sitting at the table. "Hey, Dad," he said. "Does this mean I don't get my own gym?"

32

LATER IN MY ROOM, Nicky, Tara, and I celebrated with big glasses of Coke and a bowl of tortilla chips. I made sure that my door was closed so our party wouldn't be interrupted.

"I'm not moving to Texas!" I cried, pumping my fists in the air.

I couldn't control myself. I climbed onto my bed and started leaping up and down for joy. "No Texas! No Texas! Yaaaaay!"

Tara grinned at me. "You're stuck with us, Max," she said.

I jumped up and down some more. My bed is an excellent trampoline. "You're my best friends," I said. "I didn't really want to leave you."

Nicky climbed onto my bed and tried jumping up and down too. But he kept floating too high. His head was shooting right through the ceiling.

Finally, we stopped. We slapped high fives and low fives all around.

"That spell book really works," Nicky said to Tara.

She grinned. "Did you like my meat spell, Max?" she asked. "Am I a great magician? Bringing meat to life?"

I stared at her. "Great magician? Are you kidding me? That meat thing almost *killed* me!"

Tara's grin grew wider. "I guess we owe Buster one. I had no idea the meat creature I made would become so *attached* to you!"

Nicky and I laughed at Tara's joke. But it wasn't funny. It had really been a close call.

"That spell book is dangerous," I said.

"Well, the sour milk spell worked really well," Nicky said. And then he covered his mouth. "Oops!"

I grabbed at the front of his shirt. "Sour milk spell? You mean . . . you two did that?"

Tara frowned at her brother. "Nicky, you blabbermouth. You weren't supposed to tell him."

My mouth dropped open. "You two did the milk bottle thing? And you dropped the pie on Mr. Marvin's head?"

They stared back at me and didn't answer.

"There *were* no ghouls in this house, were there!" I said. "It was you all along."

Again, they didn't answer. But their smiles gave them away.

"We had to do it, Max," Tara said finally. "We knew you'd be angry at us. But we didn't want you to leave."

I stared at them with my mouth open. "Well, that was a dirty trick. But . . . I'm home to stay," I said.

We partied some more. Then Nicky and Tara said good night and vanished.

I heard a noise outside. A car? Was Mr. Grimmus back?

I stepped over to the window and peered down at the driveway. No. No car.

I was about to turn away—when I saw a flash of black behind our tall evergreen hedge. I let out a gasp when the boy in black came into view.

What was he doing out there?

I decided I couldn't take it anymore. I had to find out who he was and what he wanted.

I flew down the stairs, half sliding down the banister. I grabbed the knob to the front door—but changed my mind.

I'll sneak up on him, I decided.

I trotted to the kitchen and went out the back door. Then I crept around the side of the house, pressing myself against the wall, keeping out of sight.

I stopped at the corner of the house and squinted into the front yard.

Yes. He hadn't moved. He was hunched behind the hedge, gazing up at my bedroom window.

"Don't move!" I shouted. I darted away from

the house, running straight to the hedge. "Don't move!"

To my surprise, the boy didn't run.

Breathing hard, I stopped across from him, on the other side of the hedge. I stared hard at his face. He had smooth skin, like a boy. But his dark eyes seemed very old.

"Who are you?" I demanded. "Why are you watching me?"

His face wrinkled as his expression turned to one of surprise. "Don't you know?" he asked. He had an old man's voice, hoarse and dry.

"Know?" I cried. "Know *what*?"

"Don't you understand?" he asked in his strange, raspy whisper. "They're going to *kill* you! They're going to *kill* you!"

TO BE CONTINUED

ABOUT THE AUTHOR

Robert Lawrence Stine's scary stories have made him one of the bestselling children's authors in history. "Kids like to be scared!" he says, and he has proved it by selling more than 300 million books. R.L. teamed up with Parachute Press to create Fear Street, the first and number one bestselling young adult horror series. He then went on to launch Goosebumps, the creepy bestselling series that gave kids chills all over the world and made him the number one children's author of all time (*The Guinness Book of Records*).

R.L. Stine lives in Manhattan with his wife, Jane, their son, Matthew, and their dog, Nadine. He says he has never seen a ghost—but he's still looking!

Be sure to check out the next book in the
Mostly Ghostly series,

Let's Get This Party Haunted!

A TERRIFYING SURPRISE PARTY . . .

MAX'S BIRTHDAY PARTY WASN'T supposed to be a
surprise. He'd planned it for weeks! He wanted to
impress his friends—especially Traci Wayne, the
girl he's a little nuts about.

But when two ghosts live in your house, *every*
party is a surprise party!

Nicky and Tara—the two ghosts who live with
Max—are angry that he didn't invite them. They
decide to turn Max's party into a SCREAM!

Poor Max has even bigger problems. He can't
shake the frightening figure in black who is following him, watching his every move. And Max
discovers a shocking secret about his new best
friend!

Happy *haunted* birthday, Max. . . .

MY NEW FRIEND, QUENTIN, came over to practice magic tricks. My party was only a few days away. I wanted to rehearse and rehearse until our act was perfect.

After all, Traci Wayne was coming. I wasn't allowed to get near her. But this was my big chance to impress her.

"Let me show you a hat trick that everyone loves," Quentin said. "Do you have a real hat I could use?"

I rubbed my chin, thinking hard. "No. I only have baseball caps," I said. "Oh, wait. My dad has a really good hat he uses for weddings and funerals and things."

"Go get it," Quentin said. "You'll like this trick."

I hesitated. "But it's my dad's only hat, and it's very expensive. You have to be very careful."

"No problem," Quentin said. "The trick is perfectly safe. I've done it a thousand times."

I went down to my parents' bedroom closet to

borrow Dad's hat. He and Mom were in the den, watching wrestling on TV. They were both shouting at the screen: "Kill him! Kill! Kill! Break him in two!"

They both love wrestling. But sometimes they get carried away. Last week after a big match, Mom jumped on Dad and started slapping his bald head with both hands. He had to pick her up and carry her into the shower to snap her out of it.

I pulled Dad's hat down from the top shelf. And I also borrowed one of his neckties. He only has three, but I don't think I've ever seen him wear one. I had learned a nifty new necktie trick that I knew Quentin would love.

"Kill! Kill! Ruin him!" My parents' shouts rang out from the den.

Back in my room, I handed Quentin the hat. "What's the trick?" I asked. "Will it be good for the party?"

He nodded. He pulled a few things from his magic kit. He held up two eggs. "I crack these two eggs into the hat," he said. "Then I pour in this jar of honey. Then I turn the hat right side up, and it's perfectly dry."

I gulped. "Are you sure about this?"

"Of course, I'm sure," Quentin said. "It's an easy trick. Watch."

He pushed his blond hair off his forehead. Then he cracked the two eggs and let them run into the hat. Then he opened the honey jar, turned it upside down, and the honey slowly oozed into the hat with the egg yolks.

"Say the magic words!" Quentin cried. "Hat be good!" He turned the hat over—and honey and yellow egg yolk came dripping out.

"You—you ruined my dad's hat!" I wailed.

Quentin squinted at the sticky mess inside the hat. "I don't get it. That trick always works."

My heart started leaping around in my chest. I shoved the hat under my bed. Later I'd have to figure out a good hiding place for it.

"What's up with the necktie?" Quentin asked, picking up the tie and pulling it through his fingers.

"Here's a good trick for the party," I said. "And this one is totally safe."

I took the tie from him and picked up a pair of scissors. "See? I make it look like I've cut the tie into four pieces. But I don't really cut it. I cut this piece of cloth instead."

I pulled the cloth from my magic kit and tucked it under the tie. "Now watch," I said. "It looks like I cut the tie up. But when I tug on it, it's all together again."

"Cool," Quentin muttered.

"Ladies and gentlemen," I boomed, holding the tie in front of me. "The Amazing Indestructible Necktie!"

I snipped it into four pieces. I balled the pieces

up in my hand. And then I gave a hard tug. "Back together again!" I exclaimed.

Wrong.

I'd sliced my dad's tie into four pieces.

"Oh, wow." I stared at the pieces of tie in my hand.

Then I pictured my dad, as big as a truck, a bellowing bull when he was angry. When he saw what I'd done to his hat and tie, he'd . . . he'd . . .

I couldn't even think about it.

Trembling, I shoved the pieces of necktie under my bed next to the hat.

Quentin tried a few easy card tricks. The cards fell from his hands and scattered over the floor. He tried the trick where he waves his magic wand and it turns into a bouquet of flowers. It didn't work. The wand broke in two.

He shook his head. "Max, everything is messed up tonight. I can't figure out why."

I could.

I knew what was happening. Nicky and Tara were messing up our tricks.

I gritted my teeth and balled my hands into fists. I felt so angry, I wanted to scream.

But *no way* could I tell Quentin about them.

Nicky and Tara were angry because they couldn't come to my party. So they were doing their best to mess up our magic act.

We tried a few more easy tricks, and they were

ruined too. "It just isn't our night," Quentin said. "Maybe we should try again tomorrow night."

He left, shaking his head, very confused.

As soon as he was out the door, my two ghost friends appeared. "How's it going, Max?" Tara asked, grinning at me.

"You *know* how it's going," I snapped.

"Did you have a bad night?" Nicky asked, acting innocent.

I realized I was grinding my teeth. I'd never been so angry at them. "You have no right to do that," I shouted. "You have no right to ruin all our tricks."

"I'll bet your tricks will go a lot better if you invite us to your party," Tara said.

"For sure," Nicky chimed in. "Invite us to your birthday party, and we'll be your best friends again."

"No way!" I cried. "You're not my best friends. Quentin is my best friend. And stop begging me. No way are you coming to my party!"

They both put on these really hurt faces. Tara pulled off her hat, tossed it on the floor, and started stomping on it.

I turned away from them and walked to the window. I took deep breaths, trying to calm down. I didn't like being angry at them. They were two poor ghosts, after all. They probably wouldn't have any more birthdays—because they were dead.

But messing up our magic tricks like that was just plain mean.

I gazed out the window, pressing my forehead against the cool glass. A few stars twinkled dimly in the night sky. I lowered my eyes—and gasped when I saw the boy in black staring up at me.

He stood at the side of my yard, leaning against a tree trunk.

I pulled up the window, stuck my head out, and shouted down at him. "Go away! I'm warning you! Go away!"

He took a few steps closer to the house. Light from the kitchen downstairs washed over him, and I saw his face. An old man's face, lined and wrinkled and sagging.

He cupped his hands around his mouth and called up to me. "Be careful!"

Gripping the windowsill, I stared down at his ancient face, at his pale, sunken eyes. "What do you want?" I screamed. "Why are you doing this?"

"Be careful," he said in a breathy rasp of a voice. "They are going to kill you. The ghosts are going to kill you!"

A chill ran down my back. I stepped away from the window. Shivering, I turned to Nicky and Tara.

"What did he mean?" I asked. "Why did he say that? Why did he say you ghosts are going to *kill* me?"

I saw the shock on Nicky's and Tara's faces.

And then they disappeared.

030